---------------- ★ ----------------

Much too soon, both cars made a quick turn into a side road that led off into the trees. I stopped there, dying to follow and debating with myself just exactly how stupid it would be. Before I could decide, there was a hand on my car door and a voice saying, "Move over, miss. You're coming with me." Before I could say, "I certainly am not," I saw the gun in his hand.

I moved over and let him drive me into the woods, to where Wishon and the other man were waiting with the two cars.

Wishon snatched off my scarf and sunglasses. "I thought it was you. Stupid bitch. Do you think we're playing 'Moonlighting' here?" He turned to the others. "She's a reporter. What do we do now?"

---------------- ★ ----------------

TRISS STEIN

MURDER AT THE CLASS REUNION

WORLDWIDE®

TORONTO • NEW YORK • LONDON
AMSTERDAM • PARIS • SYDNEY • HAMBURG
STOCKHOLM • ATHENS • TOKYO • MILAN
MADRID • WARSAW • BUDAPEST • AUCKLAND

My brother said it first:
For Mom and Dad, who always gave their
children books to read.

With love, admiration, and gratitude.

MURDER AT THE CLASS REUNION

A Worldwide Mystery/October 1995

This edition is reprinted by arrangement with Walker and Company.

ISBN 0-373-26181-0

Printed in U.S.A.

Author's Note

Since Falls City may appear to resemble a real upstate New York town, I want to emphasize that no one in this book is intended to resemble any real persons, living or dead. Furthermore, the reunion described resembles actual ones I have attended only in its pleasant aspects.

Thanks are due to Byrgen Finkelman and Janet Barnett, for infomation on adoption, and to Pete McAfee, for information on law enforcement on the Thousand Islands Bridge. Any error or improbabilities are, of course, my own.

Thanks beyond words to Millie Marmur, an agent beyond my wildest dreams. To Bob, Miriam, and Carolyn, love and appreciation always.

ONE

Saturday morning

I SAT IN the cramped passenger section of a twelve-seat plane, flying north, looking down at a landscape I had not seen in twenty years. Though the magazine article in front of me was written by a colleague and I wanted to see if I could have done it better, I could not concentrate; thoughts of the last time I flew this route kept intruding. Then I was on my way south, to make a connection at LaGuardia for a flight to Boston, to college, to the great world where I planned to stay forever. My kind, dim, dreary parents, already middle-aged when I was born, would be retired and settled in a trailer park in Florida by Thanksgiving. They would have been my only reason, and a weak one at that, to return. With a sigh, I gave up on the article, put the magazine away, and concentrated on the rolling dairy country, deep summer green, so far below.

As late as last night I had not been sure I would make this trip at all, and I was still wondering just why I was on the plane. For days now, ever since I picked up my ticket, my mind had been flooded with high-school memories . . . faces, names, incidents, personalities. Standing at the edge of all of them, as she'd been at the edge of high-school life, was a girl with flyaway, uncontrollable hair and clothes that were always wrong, who was too tall, too skinny, too serious, too smart. Me.

Below me now, the highway went straight north, straight as a dark ruler laid down over the land. To my left there was the curving line of the lake shore and the dark sparkling expanse of Lake Ontario. I used to think it was as big as the ocean, back in the days when I had never seen an ocean. Now I had seen them all except the Antarctic.

I looked at my watch, thought, "Only ten more minutes," and closed my eyes.

The mimeographed invitation to my twentieth high-school reunion had found me at my office. No one in my hometown knows where I live now, but I write for *News Now*, that highly successful national magazine that's a cross between *Time* and *Life*. I suppose someone from my class saw my name in it and took a chance that I am the same Kay Engels. Everyone knew I wanted to be a journalist. I glanced at the description of the party, the list of "lost" classmates with my name on it, and thought, That'll be the day. But I tossed it into the back of a drawer instead of the wastebasket; and one day, idly doodling during an important telephone interview, I realized with astonishment that I was drawing a map of Falls City's central square and main streets. Maybe it's time to go back after all, I said to myself, and went to see my editor about turning it into an assignment. The only way I would ever consider going was as a cool professional. Then it wouldn't matter if I had a terrible time, because I wouldn't really be there at all. I would only be on assignment, an observer and recorder.

Howard's first response was, "It's a trite idea, a cliché. They even used it in a Superman movie. Come on, Kay! Show me how your reunion story will be different from anyone else's!"

"Because my *class* wasn't like anyone else's." Inspiration came as I talked. "Think about it. We were the Vietnam generation. Some of us went off to war, and some of us went off to college where we protested the war. It's cast-in-concrete Republican country. What did Watergate do to that? Or the women's movement? What changes did this *particular* twenty years bring?" As he still hesitated, I added with a smile, "You know stories about trends are usually talking about big cities. What about all the Falls Cities? Do people there do aerobics and eat blackened redfish?"

He laughed at that and said yes. Leaving his office, I realized that in convincing him I had also convinced myself. There was a possible story there.

Nevertheless my heart sank along with my stomach when the plane landed in the hometown I couldn't wait to leave twenty years ago. I said to myself, quite sternly, "I am a woman of the world and a reporter, and I can handle this reunion, or anything." Remembering Howard's comment, I added, "Lois Lane has nothing on me."

Half an hour later, after picking up my rental car, I was driving down a typical, even stereotypical, strip of motels and fast-food restaurants—Pizza Hut, Howard Johnson's, Friendly's, and more. I made my first mental note right then and there. We didn't even have a McDonald's when I lived here. I checked into the big new Sheraton Inn that had been built right downtown on the site of a once-splendid old hotel. There were a few messages for me: from my office, asking me to confirm the source of a quote; from a man I dated casually, reminding me that he'd meet my return flight; and one that said only, "Welcome home, Kay. I always knew you'd come back someday." It was unsigned.

The young woman at the desk agreed it was strange, but said quickly, "I took that call and I really didn't forget to write it down. I remember it was a man, and when I asked him for his name he hung up, just like that. I thought I'd better give you the message anyway."

"Yes, of course," I said, shrugging. "Maybe he just had to get off the phone all of a sudden. Perhaps I'll find out at the party."

I bought a local paper at the shop in the lobby for some quick background reading after I unpacked. The room was too small, with two big beds, not enough work space, and mass-produced cheeriness, but it was clean, bright, and comfortable, about what I expected.

The paper was better than I remembered, with solid, professional writing. The stories were about the same, though. There was a two-car accident on Route 12. The football coach was optimistic about next year's varsity team. The lifeguards from the state parks on the lake were training for state-wide competition. Some children were involved in a serious accident playing with their father's gun, and one was in critical condition at County Hospital. Now here was something unusual: "Elderly woman plans to will family farm to Indians, saying it was all stolen from them originally." There seemed to be some kind of vocal conservation group on the St. Lawrence River. And there was actually one big piece of news, which I picked up from a well-written article, apparently one of a series. The army base, used only for summer training of reservists since the end of World War II, was being upgraded to a fort, giving it permanent status and putting it into full-time, year-round operation. That's a story in itself, I thought. There will be as many soldiers at Fork Oake next year as there are people in this whole town. That will bring big change. I made another mental note.

I really needed a walk after the cramped plane trip. I suddenly wanted to see if there was still a small green oval of a park in the center of the downtown square, with war memorials at either end and a wonderfully absurd silvery Victorian fountain in the middle. They used to light up the fountain at night with colored lights, and it was a special treat when I was very small to be taken downtown after bedtime to see it. I wanted to see what changes there had been in the stores, restaurants, and offices around the square that formed the central business district; to see if the terrifying traffic pattern of numerous lanes and merging streets had been improved at all.

Instead, on a sudden impulse I turned away from the square, walking up one of the broad streets that radiated out to the residential neighborhoods.

Just beyond the square there was a section of splendid Victorian houses built by the town's first rich men, in the preautomobile days when a house near the center of town was a sign of prestige. By my childhood, the movement was already outward, toward the edge of town. Families with money built large ranch houses on a hill at the town boundaries, and many of the beautiful old homes were now offices. Not all, though. I could see that some were clearly still private homes, kept up with care and, apparently, love. Or at least pride.

Beyond those streets was a section of smaller homes, equally Victorian but much less splendid, dark and poky even when built and definitely not improved with time. Not really a slum ever, but a neighborhood dreary and rundown even in my childhood, and, I saw, much the same now. Perhaps a little more worn-out. I had lived on one of these streets.

I remembered that dark front living room. I realized now for the first time that it must have had antiquated electrical wiring. The bathroom had an old pitted linoleum floor and an enormous stained bathtub with clawed feet. I smiled, thinking about how valued these old tubs are in my brownstone New York neighborhood, how painstakingly restored. I used to long for pastel porcclain. My parents never understood why.

As I turned the corner to my old block, I saw with astonishment that all the houses were gone, replaced by a long, low, cinder-block strip of businesses: a pizza place, a video games gallery, a liquor store, and—as nearly as I could work it out—a laundromat where my house used to be.

I had wondered what I would feel when I saw the house. I certainly did not expect nostalgia. Would it be a flashback to my childhood sense of suffocation in my mother's knick-knack-cluttered, furniture-stuffed rooms? I remembered, for the first time in years, the room I had made for myself my last year in high school and my mother's increasing perplexity as I pulled down the frilly curtains, put the mattress on the floor, threw away all the dolls, never played with since I learned to read, and painted the entire room white.

Poor mom, I thought. Even then we were strangers. I guess we always were. Thinking about how satisfying that light-filled, austere room was, I did feel a moment of nostalgia for the girl I had been. I was a tough cookie even then.

But now, as I stared at the laundromat, I felt deflated. All the turmoil of emotion I felt walking there led to this—a completely strange street about which I could feel nothing? It served me right for being a sentimental fool, I thought, and told myself to get back to work.

I returned to the square by a different route to take a look at the newspaper building, a sooty red-brick pile with a working press visible in the huge front window. I remembered standing there as a child, fascinated, as the enormous sheet of newsprint flew through the machinery and magically came out as an infinite stream of newspapers.

But when I reached the spot I remembered so clearly, around the corner from the Greek-columned Masonic Lodge, there was a new bank with a plaque attached to one wall: "Here stood for 75 years the home of the *Falls City Record*. The *Record* hopes to serve the community from its new home on Talcott Street for at least another 175." I walked the two blocks to Talcott Street and found a sparkling new building with a display of old photographs and new charts in the window labeled, "Fort Oake Then, Now, and in the Future."

I was thoroughly disoriented. I couldn't remember what used to be here. Some local shops? Another bank? J.C. Penney? Or was this the old Woolworth building? I felt like a fool. Only I could change. All this was supposed to be just the same, the photo I'd been holding in my mind all these years. It looked like the life of the town had gone right on without me. Why didn't I expect that?

TWO

As I walked into the hotel, I heard a voice that seemed familiar. A woman in a pink Izod shirt and sharply creased madras-plaid Bermuda shorts, with sunglasses perched on her auburn hair, was talking to the hotel manager. As I approached she broke off her conversation and, looking up, said warmly, "It's Kay, isn't it? Kay Engels?"

"Yes. And aren't you Sue Rock?"

"Yes, it's Sue Campbell now. I'm so glad you came! I saw your name on the list. Have you had lunch? My house is turned upside-down by a cleaning crew, so I'm trying to stay away," she said in an excited rush. "Would you like to join me for lunch? We're finished here, aren't we, Jack?" She turned back to me. "We were just going over final details for tonight. How about lunch?"

I said, "Okay. Where to?" thinking, why not? It's research.

Sue went on, "I've had the most incredible craving for a Leone's pizza. I haven't been there in years. It must be all this thinking about old times all week! What do you think?"

"Leone's! Is it still there?"

"Certainly is, and just as popular as ever. It's always crawling with high-school and community-college kids. We never go, because it makes us feel—"

"Out of place?"

"Worse! Old, as in 'parents,'" Sue laughed. "Our two eldest are teenagers now, and they'd just die if we showed up there. Come on, then, my car's right outside."

As we got in Sue turned to me with a delighted smile and said again, "I'm so glad you came! I think it's going to be a great reunion. About half the class is coming. Can you believe that? I remember you very well. Do you remember me at all?"

Oh, yes, I thought, I remember you. You were one of those girls who seemed to have everything and belong everywhere. And in spite of that, you were nice enough so that I always wanted to know you better.

"Of course I do," I said. "You were important in the class, a cheerleader and dance chairman, and most something-or-other."

"Oh yes, most popular. I pretty much danced my way through high school and college, but," she smiled wryly, "I did finally grow up enough to wish that I had been more like you. I guess I always did."

I could not have been more astonished if she had said she always wanted to be Albert Schweitzer. "Why in the world did you want to be like me?"

"You were smart. You had some kind of interesting life ahead of you, whatever it turned out to be. I could see that, dimly anyway, even then. You kind of went your own way and I knew you were going *somewhere*."

I was so surprised, I did something even more surprising, and told the truth. "If I did go my own way, it was only because I couldn't figure out how to do anything else. If I'd had any choice at all about it, I probably would have been you."

"Being me was easy. I just giggled a lot and pleased everyone and never let on that I had any brains." She smiled. "I did have a lot of fun, but the most original thing I could think of to do was date a succession of Italian boys whose parents ran restaurants and groceries. They were sweethearts, all of them, but not *exactly* what my parents had in mind for me. Not one of 'our crowd,' they'd say."

I dimly remembered that Sue used to live in one of those big ranch houses on the edge of town and that her father was a prominent something-or-other.

I said slowly, "What my parents had in mind for me was a job at a local store, like my mother, or... probably the height of their ambition... a secretary's job at the plant where my father worked. They developed that idea when I started making the honor roll in junior high. By the time my teachers were talking about Barnard or Radcliffe they were totally lost, like turkeys who had hatched out a parrot. So," I shrugged, "I pretty much made my own life. How about you? I take it that you live here."

"Oh, yes, and actually it turned out fine. I married Chris Campbell right after college, and we have four sons."

"Chris Campbell," I said softly, remembering him all too well. "What a nice guy he was. Very bright, and cute, too."

"I never thought so then," Sue said with a laugh. "That's probably because his parents were friends of my parents. He was just what my parents had in mind. I thought he was dull as dust, and he thought I was a perfect bubblehead."

"How did you ever get together?"

"We ran into each other the summer after junior year in college, and somehow everything seemed different then. I ended up pleasing my parents after all, by pleasing myself. It's been a good life, really. Chris is a great husband and the kids are terrific. When I started feeling—oh, housebound, I guess I'd call it—several years ago, I took on some serious community involvement, and that gave me the outlet I needed. Chris really pushed me to do it. I know you're a career woman," she concluded uncertainly. "Does that sound silly to you?"

"Not really," I said. "No one's decisions about her life will be exactly like anyone else's." But I thought that it would be living death for me.

"You know, Kay, in all those years we were in school together, we never had a real conversation. What wasted opportunities. I always wanted to talk to you more, but I was afraid I wouldn't have anything to say that wasn't dumb.''

"The funny thing is," I said, "I always had a hunch you had brains you weren't using.''

"I did, but I was getting everything a high-school girl wants without them. By the time I finally admitted I liked learning I was already engaged and on my way home. Not that I vegetated here," she added quickly. "Thank goodness I married a man who wouldn't let me! If I hadn't, I doubt we would be having this conversation and I'm glad we finally did."

"So am I," I said truthfully, somewhat surprised at how much I was liking this friendly, frank person I had envied and scorned twenty years ago.

"Kay, can you come for cocktails before the dance? We're having a few local people and some who are in from out of town, all classmates, and spouses or dates or whatever."

"I didn't bring a spouse or whatever. I was divorced two years ago."

"Doesn't matter one bit. Lots of people are coming alone. There have been a rash of divorces lately, and I hear that some out-of-town spouses refused flat-out to come, on grounds of terminal boredom. So you will come, won't you? Five-thirty and we'll join the cocktail hour at the dance about seven."

It took me by surprise, and though I wasn't sure I wanted to I ended up saying yes.

"Here we are," Sue said, starting to turn in to the parking lot but stopping at the curb. "Oh, there's

Laurie McDowell." She hit the horn and a very trim blonde looked up from opening the door of an old Chevy. "Hi, Laurie."

"Hi, Sue. I've just been across the street at the florist, checking out the bill for the decorations."

"How do they look? The decorations, I mean, not the bills."

"Oh, fine, I guess."

"Everything's shaping up," Sue went on. "I think it will be terrific. I can't wait!"

"I can." Laurie looked away. "I *was* looking forward to it, but some reunions just shouldn't happen at all." She slammed the car door and drove away fast.

Sue raised her eyebrows, but only said, "Do you remember her? She used to be Laurie Foster. Married Richie McDowell. They were together even then." She looked as if she'd like to say more but seemed to change her mind. "Let's go eat."

In a town where nearly every bar and most restaurants served some form of pizza, and had for fifty years, Leone's was the best. The owner, with children, nieces, and nephews at the high school, used to welcome teenage crowds, and the place was a popular hangout. I never went there regularly, but I supposed I had been there once or twice in my high-school days.

Now, at lunch, it was almost deserted. In the cool empty dimness of a night spot at noon, I could see that the place hadn't changed much. There were still formica tables and wood-patterned paneling, probably formica too, and one wall with pennants and buttons from all the county schools.

I suddenly realized I was very hungry. "I'm going to be totally reckless and have an individual pizza with everything. That ought to hold me until the dinner. How will it be, by the way?"

"Pretty good, and save some room for my appetizers, too."

"Okay. I'll be conservative. I'll tell them to leave off the pepperoni and just give it to me with mushrooms, anchovies, and double cheese."

"Sounds great. Make that two," Sue said to the waiter, "and two very cold Genesee beers. Is that okay?"

"Yes, indeed. Now this is something we couldn't do in high school," I said, sipping the cold beer that had been brought right away. "Age has some rewards."

"Right, let's hear it for the joys of adulthood."

After the pizza arrived, Sue said, "I feel like my life is an open book, right here, but I'd love to know more about yours. I can't even imagine having a career like yours. It must be very glamorous."

"Oh, yes and no." I was torn between a desire to show off and honesty. "Some of it is, but lots of it isn't. It's digging up background in the library or file rooms, or on the phone, sometimes manipulating people into talking when they don't want to, and of course lots of just sitting in front of the old typewriter—I mean word processor these days—writing when you'd rather be doing anything else. And I love it." I didn't care much for the role of interviewee, though, so I turned it back to Sue. "Tell me what you're doing now."

Delighted to be asked, as most people are, Sue described her role at the women's shelter and on the board of several children's recreational and welfare programs, and in the arts enrichment program at the local schools.

"So you see, I haven't been home waxing my kitchen floor."

"I never thought that!"

"Maybe not," Sue said shrewdly, "but you might have thought that I've spent my life poolside at the country club."

"Mmm. Maybe. What saved you from that?"

"Partly growing up, partly marrying Chris. He just expected me to be more interesting, and more useful, than that."

"He was always a do-gooder, wasn't he? Chairman of the blood drive and trick-or-treating for UNICEF, things like that."

"Right. He really cares. He just doesn't want to be someone whose whole life is work and family."

"He was a nice boy, always friendly when most boys didn't even talk to me."

"They were probably afraid of you," Sue said matter of factly. "Chris wouldn't have been."

"Afraid of me?" I said. "Wait a minute. I was afraid of *them*! Thank God we do grow up!"

I said it again, to myself, a few minutes later when two tall, tanned men in rumpled suits walked in. Former classmates, popular athletes who'd been part of Sue's old crowd, they'd come straight from the airport in search of "some people we used to know and love."

I'd never spoken to them in four years of high school, but now they greeted me with shouts, hugs, and laughter right along with Sue. We finally left when one of them swore, "I'm a born bachelor, Susie. In the great words of Hawkeye Pierce, they'll have to get me pregnant first! Now Tommy, let me tell you what it's like to work for Club Med—"

Sue winked at me and said, "Let's leave these two aging jocks to their pizza and man talk. I want all of you at my house for drinks tonight—8 Ridge Road, at five-thirty. Chris will flip when I tell him we saw you."

As we left, one of them was saying again, "I knew it. I knew we'd run into someone we knew if we went straight to Leone's."

Sue drove me back to the hotel and we parted laughing about our unexpected encounter in the restaurant. I spent what was left of the afternoon just walking around town, and it was only an hour later that I was getting dressed for the dance. I took off the smart black linen pants and black, cream, and tan silk shirt I'd worn for traveling, showered, and began putting on my battle armor and warpaint. When I was finished, my sleek, expensive haircut was glistening and my expensively made-up face glowed. I did like what I saw: a tall brunette in pale green silk with a matching stole and emerald earrings, a treasured birthday gift from an on-and-off boyfriend.

I thought I looked elegant and sophisticated, and I said out loud to my image in the mirror, "And that's just what I am, dammit. Being back here makes me feel like an imposter, but I am, really, just what I appear to be. So there!" I hoped that settled the skeptical woman looking back at me.

I added emerald green evening sandals and an embroidered satin bag and decided I was ready for anything, in spite of the knot in my stomach and my cold hands. As I checked myself one last time I took a deep breath and said, "You've talked to movie stars and presidents. You've been to much more important parties with much more important people. And you're not here to be a prom queen anyway. You're a member of the working press. Go. Do it."

Yet as I approached the house I had a whole set of butterflies, thinking about Chris. Even in high school, he had a self-confidence and steadiness that made him respected, and a casual friendliness that also made him liked. We were frequently classmates, and he treated me as pleasantly as he did anyone else who wasn't a part of his clique. That meant a lot to me then, but I watched him for years with the girls in the cable-knit sweaters and kilts, and would have given every *A* on my report card to have him really look at me just once. Funny how vivid those old memories were all of a sudden, when it had been so many years since I had even thought of him. None of the men in my life would have been a suitable escort tonight, but I was suddenly saying to myself, "Oh, why didn't I bring someone?"

I took a deep breath and rang the doorbell. Chris answered. In the dim hall light he looked just about the same. Average height, and a little stocky; maybe a little bit heavier now; blue eyes; perhaps a few lines in his face; a little gray in the light brown hair.

He stepped out, taking both my hands in his, and kissed me lightly on the cheek. "It's wonderful to see you, Kay. I haven't forgotten you in honors English class. I knew even then that you'd be somebody."

"Thank you, Chris. I'm glad to be here tonight, though I don't suppose I thought, then, that I would ever say it. All I wanted in those days was to get out."

"Well, now come in and welcome back," he said with a smile, and steered me in with a light touch on my back. "You remember Alan Levin? And Danny Williams? Vicky Kincaid? Carol Van Allen? They're all here, all the old gang. Let me get you a drink first." He led me off and I followed, thinking how strange it was that nobody but me seemed to remember that I was never a part of that gang. Or any gang.

And for the rest of the evening, no one did seem to remember or care about old gangs or old friends. Every new arrival was greeted with cries of joy and the big living room was filled with the sound of forty or so adults excitedly catching up on each other's lives. Far from drifting at the edge, as I had expected, I was immediately included and even seemed to be a bit of a celebrity.

When it was time to leave for the dance, everyone piled into several cars and I somehow found myself in someone else's crowded car, sitting on the lap of the bachelor we'd met in Leone's and discussing with him whether I still remembered how to do the twist.

THREE

AFTER WE ALL checked in, the rest of the crowd from the party laughed at the name tags with our high-school yearbook pictures on them. I shuddered and promptly buried mine at the bottom of my purse.

We entered the ballroom to the irresistible beat of "I'm a Believer." My friend from the car grabbed my hand, saying "Come on, let's show them how to do it," before I had time to protest that I never really knew how to do it. I followed his lead well enough not to make a fool of myself, and by the end of the dance, we were both gasping for breath and laughing. Other people we used to know came up to us then, and started talking. Even now, when I think of that evening, it is the sound that comes to me first, the sound that started at Sue and Chris's and continued almost to the end, the excited high-pitched buzz, punctuated by cries of "I don't *believe* it!" and "I'll be goddamned!" and all of it underlaid by an insistent rock-and-roll beat.

After the sound, the memories are like a series of snapshots, the moments that held still amid the blur of hellos and hugs, of vaguely familiar faces in the crowd, of summarizing my life again and again for people who could barely hear over the band. Some moments remained clear, sharply focused in my mind, to be re-created later in my words:

—A bearded giant who looked like a lumberjack and clearly knew me well, though I didn't recognize him at all at first. We'd only grown up on the same block for a dozen years or more. He'd run away from a vicious father after knocking him to the floor during one beating too many, and had run and run. Now at last he'd made a life for himself in the Colorado hills, building houses, hunting, and skiing. "Of course," he said, "this is after a few stops along the way in two marriages, the army, and AA. Kay, God looks after fools. That's the only explanation I can come up with for why I'm not in jail or dead. Here I am, a success-ful businessman with a good woman." He ended with a grin. "Tell me you're not surprised." And I had to admit I couldn't. It was a pleasant surprise, though, and I told him so, with a hug.

—The class cutup who told me how he'd always been a salesman, could sell anyone anything, and knew he'd take over his family's successful men's store some day. Then two years in Vietnam made selling suits just seem not important enough. "So," he concluded, "I went to work for the United Way. I'm still selling, you see, but now I'm selling services for the elderly and handi-capped and so on, selling those needs to the commu-nity. It's more satisfying than suits and ties."

—A classmate who'd gone to West Point, spent twelve years in the army, and was now a civilian con-sultant in El Salvador. No combination of charm and persistence could get more of an answer to "What do you do there?" than a bland "I consult."

I had dinner with Sue and Chris and some of the others from the party, with much seat shifting and table hopping between courses. I talked mostly to the women during dinner. Some I had known from school activities, some I had never spoken to before. None had been my friends, but I came to the reunion to listen, and everyone told me a story.

I heard about marriages happy, tolerated, and ended; and of careers successful, abandoned, and started fresh. I heard a number of women disavow being feminists, and then go on to express opinions any feminist could applaud. I saw photos of children from college age to infancy, and heard one woman, glowing in a late first marriage, confess to being pregnant for the first time at age thirty-seven, and another tell of adopting two Vietnamese toddlers when her own children were in their teens. Someone I remembered as a quiet, conventionally well-dressed, and very boring girl had metamorphosed into a highly articulate, distinctively elegant woman, a successful theatrical designer who lived ten blocks from me in New York. We talked enough to know there was much more to say, and exchanged cards and promises to meet in the city.

By this time, my cherished reporter's cool was rapidly being melted by the warmth everyone was showing. I could feel my observer's stance slipping away, but some part of my mind was still at work, as I'd intended. I began to play with the idea of not just one article about the reunion but a whole series of them, each focusing on a classmate with a different story and how that individual's story might fit into the story of the class as a whole. A mosaic, in other words. I was tossing different title possibilities around in my mind when the evening's emcee called for our attention.

Each time he spoke I thought his voice was familiar, but I could not recognize him at all. Then I closed my eyes, covered his bald head with unruly curls, subtracted thirty pounds, and recognized him as the inevitable announcer at all the pep rallies and games and school shows.

"Please, folks, we've got a whole evening of dancing and talking ahead of us, but we have to make a couple of announcements now. First, we ought to thank the committee members who worked so hard to arrange this night and contact all of us. I'll read their names, and c'mon, kids, let's get them to stand up and give them a great big hand."

As he read the names, I was distracted by a woman hurrying over to our table, smiling broadly, almost bouncing on her high heels. She was in a bright, ruffled, red-and-white dress, cut very low, with her bright blond hair swept very high. The man with her was big, very big, gray-haired, in a dark suit and silk shirt open at the neck, a large diamond ring on his right pinky. Certainly not a classmate.

When Sue sat down after being applauded for her reunion role I whispered, "Who is that woman?"

"Don't you know?" Sue said drily. "Look again."

I did look again as the woman stood up and blew Sue a kiss. I said, "That isn't Terry Campbell!"

"Certainly is," Sue answered with a grin.

Just in time, just before I said, "But she looks awful!" I remembered she was Chris's cousin, and changed my comment to "She's changed a lot, hasn't she?"

"Nope," Sue answered, "she looks now like what she always was. Of course she used to know how to dress," she added, smoothing the skirt of her own elegant pink satin dress.

I kept watching as Terry bent over the men at the table, displaying the maximum cleavage and seeming to be unable to talk to them without a caress on the cheek or a hand on the shoulder. The blond hair was brassier now than in high school and the heavy makeup didn't quite conceal lines in a complexion that used to be rosepetal perfect. At an age when most girls aspired to be cute Terry had been a genuine beauty. When most girls could not yet buy a bra without embarrassment Terry had a woman's figure and the walk to call attention to it, though her big blue eyes always seemed to deny knowing anything at all about what her body was doing. She never showed the slightest awareness of my existence, of course, but no one in our class could have been unaware of hers.

Sue leaned over to whisper to me, "We've seen her over the years. She's Chris's cousin and she breezes into town a few times a year. Even in high school she was a bit, uh, predatory, but she's gotten worse lately. She works overtime proving she still has what it takes.''

"Who's the man?''

Sue shrugged. "She's been divorced twice, and is in the courts now with the third husband. Lately she's always got a different new man. This one looks tough, doesn't he?''

Terry was with a male classmate now, her escort watching with no apparent concern as she leaned over the guy's shoulder, giggling and nuzzling his ear. He looked abashed but pleased, and was responding with a lightly stroking hand on her hip.

Watching this little scene, I couldn't resist saying, "She hasn't aged well, has she?''

"No.'' Sue smiled wickedly. "And I can't think of anyone who deserves it more.'' The emcee was speaking again, and Sue said, "Shh. I guess we'd better listen.''

"Okay, folks, I hope you're all enjoying your desserts. We'll have this fine band back in a minute to play some more evergreen greats. It's terrific, isn't it, how these twenty-year-old musicians have gotten into the sixties spirit? And if some of the songs are really early sixties, well, we were cool. We were dancing to them in sixth grade too, weren't we?

"But before they come back, I have the very pleasant job of handing out some prizes. Now this handsome trophy here is for the reunionee who traveled the farthest to get here. As far as we can tell, that would be Donny DuPont, in from his navy assignment in the

Philippines. Anyone want to dispute that? Okay, Don, come on up here and claim her, and let's all give this sailor a big hand.

"Now we have four couples here that we know of, where husband and wife were both in our class, married each other, and, believe it or not, are still married. How about that? We think these lovely ladies deserve a reward for putting up with any guy from our class for this long, so we got 'em each a nice orchid, and the husbands get a boutonniere for knowing a good thing when they see it and hanging on to it. Come on up when I read your names and if we missed any other couples, our apologies and you just come on up too."

I didn't know the first two couples, but as the third pair of names were called I did have a flash of memory. Laurie Foster and Richie McDowell. She was the woman I'd met in Leone's parking lot. In the old days she was a lively blond, all smiles and pep, a cheerleader and tennis player, and he was a big, dark-haired, handsome guy, good-natured, athletic and not much of a student. They used to win dance contests together.

She was still slim and athletic-looking, but the sparkle seemed to be gone and had not been replaced by the mature self-confidence I was seeing in so many other classmates. She looked tired and sad in what should have been her happy moment in the spotlight. I wondered what had happened to her.

As I watched them I noticed Terry looking too, with an odd smile, both scornful and amused. I searched around in memories more than twenty years old and wondered if Richie and Terry hadn't been a couple for awhile.

Sue and Chris were the last ones called. After the flowers were presented, the emcee said, "Let's let these happy couples have the dance floor to themselves as we listen to—remember this one?"

The banquet room lights went out and the couples were spotlighted as the band played "Close to You."

At this point I was ready for some air and a few minutes alone to sort out my many impressions of this evening. It was cool outdoors and blessedly quiet, with the band's sound muffled, as I strolled slowly around the pool.

"Kay!" someone called from the parking lot. "Kay! I've been waiting all evening for you to come out." I walked toward the voice, trying to see in the dim light. The speaker took a few steps toward me, saying, "I've been dying to see you. Did you get my message?" The voice was uncertain, in spite of the confident words.

I still couldn't see him very well, but my memory started clicking at last, and I finally said, "Andy? Andy Monroe? Is that you?"

He laughed and finally got close enough for me to see him in the pool lights.

"It's me. I knew you'd remember. I knew you right away, even though you've changed your hair." He blinked rapidly. "I liked it better the other way. You know. Longer. It was pretty then."

"I didn't see you at the party—"

"Oh, no, no. I'm not here at the party. I didn't feel like it. I don't really like parties all that much. But," he said in a brighter tone, "I've been watching from the parking lot. I saw you come in with a lot of people."

I took a deep breath and said gently, "Yes, Andy, I met some friends. How are you? Do you live here?"

"Oh, yes. Oh, yes. I'm used to this place. I get used to something and I don't like to change. Maybe I would have gone in the service. I tried to be a marine. I wanted to learn to use a gun, but they didn't take me. I was glad not to go away. I'm used to being here."

He stopped abruptly, as if he'd wound down. I said, "Do you have a job?"

"Sure I do! I work for the Highway Department. I work at the snowplow garage in the winter. That's a pretty important job around here, you know. And in the summer, I help on the road work. I thought maybe you'd notice my tan."

"Well, it's pretty dark out here. But you do look very fit."

"I sure am. Hey, Kay, why don't you leave and come for a beer with me? I missed you. I never should've let you leave town, way back when. We've got a lot of time to make up for."

Suddenly my hand was shaking. Andy had always been a little strange, not precisely retarded but with his own unique ideas about what was happening around him, which didn't always accord with reality as most other people defined it. This conversation, however, was reaching a whole new level of strangeness.

"Andy, I'm busy now. I'm really at this reunion to work, and I can't just leave."

"Always busy, just like before." He smiled sadly, then brightened. "Maybe another day?"

I nodded dishonestly, knowing I was leaving tomorrow.

"Okay, I'll let you off now, but you'll hear from me a lot. See you later, alligator!" With a gesture that was meant to be jaunty but didn't quite come off, he left.

I'd forgotten Andy, forgotten him as completely as if he'd never existed. Maybe he never had, for me. We went to elementary school together. He was a strange little boy, always in trouble with the teachers and not good at his work, and I despised him with the immortal attitude of good little girls toward bad little boys. Strangely enough, he seemed to admire that, and he went on admiring it as we got older. Did he ever ask me out? I couldn't remember. All I remembered was that I never thought about him at all, except for the moments he was being such a pest he couldn't be ignored, but he seemed to remember it all very differently.

I wanted to think about him later, when I could try to make sense of his words, assuming they made any sense anyway, but other events intervened and it was quite some time before I thought about Andy again at all.

FOUR

As I was returning to the banquet room someone said softly, "Kay Engels, you look much too sophisticated to be in this crowd." I turned and saw, leaning against a wall, arms folded, all alone, a thin, dark-haired, dark-eyed man in the best-tailored suit I had seen so far up here in polyester land.

"So do you, Tony," I said. "What are you doing here anyway? Didn't you get sent off to prep school somewhere along the way?"

He gave a kind of half-smile I remembered very well. "What you probably never heard was that I got kicked out in disgrace. I finally graduated from Falls City High a year after all of you." He leaned over and whispered, "Promise not to tell anyone. I'm a spy. I'm reunion chairman, and I'm here to see how we can outdo you."

I couldn't imagine the cynical, standoffish Tony I used to know as reunion chairman. "Have you turned rah-rah in your old age?"

"Not me."

"Old? Or rah-rah?"

"Both, of course, but I live here now. I was asked to help out, and I figured, what the hell? During my married years I learned all about giving parties."

I said, carefully, "That sounds as if your married years are all over."

"Yes, we were divorced four years ago. How about you? Husband and kids?"

"No, I'm divorced too."

He looked at me thoughtfully for a moment, and then said, "Maybe we can exchange war stories sometime. For now, let's dance."

Dancing to "Good Vibrations," "Surfin' Safari," "Satisfaction," and "Hey Jude," I caught a glimpse, among the other dancers, of Richie McDowell and Terry dancing too slowly, too tightly, in a dark corner, and I thought briefly that there was something more than old times' sake there, but then the dance was ending, and when the music stopped, Tony was still holding my hand.

With another half-mocking, quizzical look, he said, "Why don't we find a quiet corner of the garden and tell each other the story of our lives?"

I felt myself smiling a bit too brightly and answering in a voice that was a little hard, "Mine is more of a cross between 'Brenda Starr, Reporter' and a soap opera."

He gave me that considering look again and then suddenly, with a real smile of unexpected charm, tucked my hand under his arm and said, "I suspect mine resembles most of the characters in 'Doonesbury,' all jumbled up together. Come on, we'll draw each other some comic strips."

So we sat in the cool, quiet courtyard garden surrounding the pool, under a perfect starry sky, and I told him about how glad I had been to get away, about college and work and how it had changed me and what it had given me. I had been uncomfortable talking about myself to Sue; now it was easy.

"When I was at Radcliffe I got a job as a campus reporter for the *Globe*. That was a lucky break—what was happening on the campuses then was big news, and I was in just the right place a couple of times. Those stories got me a job with the *Times* when I graduated, and after that I did a bit of everything—general assignment, city hall. Spent five years overseas, including the Middle East."

"Did you get to wear a mysterious slouch hat and one of those foreign correspondent trench coats? I could see you in that."

I had to smile. "Well, in London, of course. It's a job requirement. Not in the Middle East, in that heat!"

"Sounds like it was an exciting time."

"It was, but the Middle East tour left me really burned-out. When I came back and *News Now* offered me a job I jumped at the chance. They send me where they need me if there's a news story, but I also get to do more extended pieces."

"So you really did turn into Brenda Starr?"

I had to smile again. "Yes, my girlhood dreams came true...except for the red hair."

Arms stretched out along the bench, looking up at the sky, he asked, "Aren't you leaving something out?"

"My marriage," I said through a suddenly tightened throat. "Yes. He was—is—another writer. We were thirty-two, old enough to know what we were doing. And we'd been living together a couple of years in Europe.

"I don't know. I keep trying to tell it like a well-written story, with a strong lead and a neat, witty wrap-up, but when I do it like that I'm always faking. The truth is, I *don't* know. He started a book and began keeping regular hours, and I was still traveling a lot, and more successful all the time. He didn't like that. He wanted me to quit, and start a book, and be like him. I thought it was insufferable and bullying of him, then. Now I wonder if maybe he was just feeling...neglected...maybe too far down in my priorities. Maybe he was right. We had a couple of rocky years and then," I concluded in a small voice, "he found someone who made him first in her life. We were divorced two years ago."

Without looking away from the sky, he took my hand. "Any kids?"

"No," I said softly. "Maybe I regret that, maybe not. It's just one more thing about my life I don't know. When we were married, it was one of the many things to fight about. It was never the right time for both of us. I guess it's just as well, as things turned out."

Still looking up, he asked casually, "Seeing any-one?"

"I see a lot of two men." I surprised myself with a burst of complete honesty. "They're both completely wrong for me."

Then he did look at me, and smiled, and said, "Of course. That makes it a dead certainty you can't get involved with either."

"Thank you very much, Dr. Sigmund Campbell," I said, pulling my hand away and folding my arms. "Now what about you? Start with what the hell you're doing back here, and why."

"*What* is easy. Practicing law. *Why* is a little less precise."

"When last heard of, our hero had been thrown out of prep school, and, finally achieving a high-school diploma somewhat late went on to—what?"

"Cornell, strictly on the basis of my SAT scores and some no-doubt-lying recommendations written by well-placed cronies of my father. I couldn't have gotten into Podunk State on my grades alone. I think I went there with the idea of getting kicked out, but couldn't seem to pull it off."

"It can't have been that difficult. Perhaps you weren't giving it your full attention."

"That's true." He grinned. "I actually had some good teachers there, and for the first time in my life, really challenging work. Every time I tried serious hell-raising—not the ordinary college-boy stuff—"

"Drinking till you passed out on Saturday night?"

"Right. I did some of that, and discovered social drugs too. No, I mean the big stuff that could actually have got me kicked out, I'd somehow get sidetracked by an interesting paper or a lecture by someone too good to pass up. I was kind of embarrassed about it, but I ended up graduating with honors."

"Come on! I bet you loved it."

"I did. Sure. But I still ran with a bad crowd when I was home. One guy ended up in jail, and at least two wrecked themselves on drugs. It took me a while to face up to the fact that I didn't need them anymore. The answer ended up being to stop coming back. Maybe the very best thing about college was that it got me away from here."

"Do I hear an echo?"

He smiled. "But I had a long line of distinguished ancestors to live up to, founding fathers of the town; an important father; Chris Campbell, my perfect cousin; Terry Campbell, my beautiful one—yes, you'd forgotten that, hadn't you?—*and* an English mother who thought Anthony sounded aristocratic. Getting into trouble was perfect. I could embarrass all of them at once. That's probably why I stopped getting into trouble when I went away."

"Maybe obscurity had its good points after all."

"You bet. That's what I found out when I went to a college where no one knew me or my family."

"After that, law school?"

He nodded. "Law school, since I was blessed with a high draft-lottery number. I went to Columbia and

swung between antiwar demonstrations and making
A's in corporate law. I ended up with a big-bucks job
at a Wall Street firm and became a so-called success in
spite of myself.''

"What was it you said to me? 'Aren't you leaving
something out?'"

"I was getting around to it," he said, sounding
amused. "I met my wife the first week of my last year
in law school, and I'd say she had a lot to do with my
going to Wall Street. I was crazy about her, and that
was the kind of life she wanted. At least, she liked the
money and the prestige. By the time we'd been married seven or eight years, and she realized partners
make a lot more money than associates but still put in
sixty-hour weeks, she was getting very, let's say, fidg-
ety. She's very social. That's how I developed my pre-
viously mentioned party expertise, but I wasn't actually
around to party as much as she would have liked. We
stumbled along for a few more years, but she finally
picked up the kids and went back to Grosse Pointe and
mummy and daddy. I believe she thought she'd find a
playmate who didn't have to work for a living.''

"Did she?"

"Oh, yes, eventually. To make something complex
sound very simple, all of a sudden I had no reason to
be in New York anymore. So, I came home to see if I
could find something to do here that made sense. My
folks live near Palm Beach a good nine months of the
year now and even when they're up for the summer,
they're out at the lake. I have my own life here and I

don't see much of them. They sold the big family house when they moved, and I was still in New York, telling them I'd come back when hell freezes over. Now I'm actually thinking about trying to buy it back, to convert it into some nice apartments with one for myself. So, things change. I can drive to Detroit to see my kids in less time than it takes from New York, and there are Detroit flights into Syracuse. I feel closer to them here than I did in the city.''

"But I still don't understand how you can do it after a life in New York! Who do you talk to? Aren't you bored?''

"Stick around and I'll show you. It's very different, but I was ready for—badly needed—a change. Care to go sailing tomorrow? I have a cottage at Point Pleasant and a very fine little boat.''

I said, "I'm sorry. I'm leaving at eleven tomorrow. I would have loved it.'' And I meant it.

"Too bad,'' he said. "Too bad we never knew we were both in New York, too. On the other hand, I'm coming down next month on business. What would you say to dinner?''

Though the suggestion was casual enough, I was surprised and disturbed at how happy it made me. Something seemed to be happening, and much too fast. I searched my mind for an answer to lighten up the mood, and finally said, "I would say, your American Express card or mine?''

"Is that a smart-ass way of saying yes?''

I nodded.

He said, "It occurs to me that we're wasting an evening talking. We ought to be in there reuniting and dancing our feet off, or we ought to be out here necking under the stars."

I giggled and started to answer when we both became aware that someone else was nearby, hidden in the darkness and shrubbery and talking in intense whispers. A woman's voice, thick with liquor or passion, was saying, "Come on, honey, say you will. You've got to want to as much as I do. I've been thinking of you all the time since Christmas. I can't stand seeing you and not touching."

A man, voice as husky as the woman's, responded. "We can't. It's too risky. They're right here. How can we get away with it? You know I want to."

We looked at each other, appalled but pinned to the spot, knowing there was no way we could leave without the other couple seeing us.

We heard murmuring and moaning, and then the woman's voice again.

"We can go back in by the parking-lot door. No one will even see us! Please, baby, please—"

Groaning, he said, "Yes. All right. Yes. You've got the key? I can't ever say no to you. I always want you too much."

We heard footsteps, and then in the moonlight we saw a man's broad, dark back and a flash of red-and-white ruffles. Tony was gripping my hand so hard it hurt.

He said in an even, angry monotone, "That bitch. My cousin Terry."

"You're sure?"

"Absolutely. Aren't you?"

I nodded.

"Got a damn good idea the guy was Richie Mc-Dowell. Did you see them dancing?"

She nodded. "He was half of one of those happy reunion couples."

"That's it," he said grimly. "They had a fling in the old days and I've always thought she still kind of had him on a string. Worse. You know those toys, wooden paddles with a little ball attached to a long rubber band? That's Richie, Terry's bouncing ball, not able to go any further than she lets him."

"You sound awfully bitter. Did she ever do that to you?"

"Hell, no! One thing Chris and I do have in common is that we're immune to little Terry's maneuvers. We grew up with her, don't forget, and we know exactly who she really is. She could always fool the grown-ups, and all the guys, of course, but it just doesn't work on us. She hates us for it, of course," he added matter-of-factly. "No, my bitterness is guilty conscience. Her first husband was a college friend of mine. I introduced them, and she made his life miserable for a very long time."

"Oh, come on, Tony. It couldn't have been all her fault. She's not a witch. He could have left her if he was so miserable. Why didn't he?"

"He loved her, at first. Maybe later it was habit, or need, or she convinced him she'd be suicidal. Who the hell knows? Maybe it's still love. She left him, finally, and he never did get over it, poor bastard. Oh, hell, let's drop it. It makes necking out here less appealing, though, doesn't it? Let's go dance."

FIVE

IN THE BANQUET ROOM everyone was dancing and singing to "My Girl," and then the band took a break and we mingled, drifting from group to group. I couldn't help looking around for Terry's date and Laurie, Richie's wife. I told myself it was my reporter's instinct for getting the whole story, but I suspected, deep down, that it was just nosiness. Still, I looked. Terry's date seemed to be spending the evening at the bar, quietly, steadily drinking, walking out from time to time and then returning to the bar. Laurie was with a group of women, talking animatedly, but with a haunted expression I still remember. Finally, she seemed to excuse herself and went out toward the lobby.

Somehow, I found myself walking hand in hand with Tony, and liking it, and not quite liking that I liked it. At one point, Susan caught my eye and winked. I turned to Tony and said, "Have you become my date for the prom?"

"How about that. Wait. Stay right here." He walked over to the nearest table and snapped some flowers from the centerpiece. "Here's your corsage. Sorry they were all out of wristband orchids," he said with a grin.

I had to smile. "I think I can just tuck them in here." I slid the scratchy stems into the bodice of my dress, and added, "But darn it, I wanted one of those clear plastic boxes so I could keep it in the refrigerator all week. I never did have one of those," I was getting giddy and I didn't care.

"I think I ought to join Sue and Chris for a while. Do you mind?"

"I never mind Sue. Let's see. He's not in sight. Good. We'll go talk to Sue."

Before we could make our way across the dance floor Sue came toward us, linked arms with me, and said with a grin, "Come to the powder room with me. We can try each other's lipsticks and talk about our dates."

Crossing the lobby, out of a corner of my eye, I noticed Terry's date talking at the phone booth, but I was too far away to hear him. I didn't say a word to Sue, and finally she said to me, "Dates, Kay. We're talking about dates, remember? What's going on?"

"I don't know. I didn't start out with a date, and didn't expect one and—"

"And? And?"

I finally said, "I'm having a wonderful time! It makes me nervous."

Sue hugged me and said, "Don't be silly. I just knew you were having fun. Tony's a bit prickly around the edges, but there's a good person inside. He and Chris don't like each other, but," she shrugged, "they'll grow up, and out of it, someday."

While we were repairing our makeup, I asked, "What about the McDowells?"

Sue raised her eyebrows. "Oh? You saw something?"

I nodded.

Sue said, "Yes, I did too. Half the class saw them dancing. Wasn't it awful? I wonder if that's what she meant when we saw her this afternoon.

"I think I really, truly, don't want to know if there was anything else. I mean, I do want to know, but I see Laurie every so often. The less I know, the less I can blab by accident. All I know is that they live here, they're both gym teachers, three kids, not much money. What else?"

"Are they happy?"

"Doesn't look it, does it? There are rumors. She looks so depressed and oh, anxious. I think that's the word I want. Worried." Sue shook her head. "Do you remember her in high school? She was the perfect little cheerleader, out there during football games in November, with the snow starting and her knees turning blue in those short skirts, and she never stopped smiling. I can't remember when I last saw her smiling." She sighed. "Oh, well, none of us are young and carefree, but don't you think most of us have aged well? How do we seem to you after all this time?"

"Mellow and improved by age, mostly. And a lot friendlier and warmer than when we were in our teens. Actually, this is so much fun, I'm going to have a hard time making a story out of it!"

Tony was waiting for me where I had first seen him, leaning against a wall next to the doorway, looking amused. The band was playing "Light My Fire," and he said, "Dancing to this music makes me feel as if I should be asking you to go out after for french fries and a milk shake and a drive up Cemetery Road."

"What in the world for?"

"Kay, didn't you ever go parking in high school? Cemetery Road was the best place. No cops, lots of privacy, and *very* quiet."

"Oh, to think of the culinary and sexual thrills I missed."

"I assure you, it could be quite thrilling. I remember—" He stopped and grinned. "No, I won't bore you with that. Would a cynical older woman like you care to dance a few more times?"

The band was playing mostly slow tunes now, the kind meant for tight dancing in the dark corners of the gym. I remembered the music, but not the dancing. I wondered if I ever danced with anyone at all in high school. Probably not. Then I just closed my eyes and let the music wash over me. They played, "You've Really Got a Hold on Me," and "Sunshine of Your Love," and "Try a Little Tenderness," and Tony and I did drift to the dark corners of the room. I thought I was being stupid. I was just letting something happen. I wasn't in charge and I didn't like it. But I just continued to drift with the music, and when they played "You've Lost That Lovin' Feelin'," I somehow found myself dancing very slowly, my arms around Tony's neck and his arms locked around my waist. When the song ended he gave me another of those questioning looks, as if we had just been talking about something, and I said, without ever actually making up my mind to do it, "If the sailing offer is still open, I'll try to change my flight."

He smiled. "Are you sure I can't interest you in a shake and fries, too?"

Before I could think of an adequately crushing reply, a young man in a desk attendant's uniform came up to Tony and said, "Are you Mr. Campbell? We have a message for you."

Tony read the pink slip he was handed and made a face. "Cousin Terry. She's sick and called the desk to find me. Strange. Guess I'd better go, but I'll be right back." He was still holding my hand. "Where will I find you? Never mind. I'll find you." He gave my hand a quick squeeze and was gone.

Feeling considerably more alone than I did at the beginning of the dance, I told myself to get back to work and began circulating, talking, informally interviewing, taking mental notes. Half an hour later I realized Tony still had not returned. Wondering if there might be a real problem, I got Terry's room number at the desk, noticing it was near mine, down a long corridor and around the corner at the far end of the building.

As I approached, I heard pounding and shouting.

"Tony," I called. "What is it? What's wrong?"

"Kay? Thank God! Go and get someone on the staff to open this door. I'm locked in—the lock's been jammed somehow—and there's trouble here."

A few minutes later the manager and I knew what trouble Tony had found: Terry Campbell Townsend Weston O'Neill, Best Looking in Her Class, was dead, strangled in her bed while her classmates danced a few hundred yards away.

SIX

"TONY, WHAT IN THE—?"

Tony, ashen-faced, held up his hand. "I'll tell you, but first we have to call the police. The phone wire's been cut. And an ambulance, I guess, though it's much too late. I did mouth-to-mouth for twenty minutes, CPR, but she was gone before I came in."

"I'll call from my office," the manager said. "Do you want to come with me?"

"I'll wait in the garden," Tony said wearily. "I need the air. Don't worry. I'll be here when the police come."

I went out with him and waited, not too patiently, while he leaned back against a tree with his eyes closed. Finally he opened them and said, "I owe you an explanation. I kind of deserted you on the dance floor, didn't I?"

"You don't owe me, but I do wish you would tell me what happened."

"I don't know. I got that message and went into Terry's room. The door was unlocked and she was sprawled on the bed, naked. I thought she'd passed out until I went over to see what I could do. And then the door slammed shut behind me and I was locked in and the phone wires were cut. I'd been yelling and pounding for about half an hour before you came along. Thank God you did! What made you, anyway?"

Was I going to say I missed him? Certainly not. "I thought there must be a problem."

He gave me the ghost of a smile. "The understatement of the century."

The manager was beckoning to Tony and I went along, determined to stay until I got kicked out. I had found my story.

Two ridiculously young uniformed policemen were there, and an older, heavy, hawk-faced man in blue jeans and a sports shirt.

"Hello, Tony," he said. "Now what the hell's going on here?"

Tony told him his story and introduced me in the process of explaining how he got out of the room. Chief LaForge looked grim by the time the story was finished.

"Hell of a thing this is, hell of a thing." He glanced down the hall toward the ballroom. The cheerful sounds of the Ronettes drifting back toward us made a bizarre background. "I've got to tell all those folks, too. Who'd be her next of kin? Husband?"

"No, she was with a date."

The chief winced. "Got to tell him too. Can you point him out to me?"

"I can," Tony said, "and I guess I'm the closest relative she's got—had—in town, along with Chris Campbell. We're both her cousins. Her parents are out at the lake."

"Okay. You stay here. Hey, you, Harrington, take their statements. Davis, you know Chris Campbell? Light-haired fellow? Local bigwig? Get him and the deceased's date and bring them to the manager's office. I want the manager, too."

"Right here."

"We need your office, don't know for how long, and I want the kid who brought Tony the message. Ask if anyone else who works here might have been down around the room tonight. And I've got to call an ambulance and the coroner. She sure is dead, and she sure was killed. Shit. Haven't had a murder in fifteen and a half years, and that one was only manslaughter. Woman shot her lover in a rage, and both drunker'n skunks." He turned back to Tony. "We'll have to seal the room. You got any reason to go back in there?"

We were all standing in the hall, but I wasn't going to let my last opportunity to see the room pass by. I stepped in quickly, ignoring Tony's "Don't. It's awful," and the chief's "Hey, you've got to stay out of there."

I said, "Tony, I've seen bodies before," and it was true. I had. I'd seen accident victims and murder victims and bombing victims, but not someone who I had seen alive, dancing and flirting and whispering in the dark, only an hour earlier. In just a moment, before the chief firmly led me out, I saw enough to write a description, but I had to clench my teeth hard while I looked.

While the chief called the ambulance and the doctor who served as county coroner, the young policeman took Tony's statement. Tony didn't mention what we'd seen in the garden, and I wondered why, but I waited. I would tell it myself, if necessary, when the right moment came.

"Yes, doc," he said with some annoyance. "Yes, there's no doubt she was killed." Pause. "How the hell do I know? That's your job."

The other policeman came in with Chris and Sue Campbell, who looked worried and puzzled, and Terry's date, impassive as ever.

"Look, folks," the chief began, "I'd give anything not to have to tell you this, but there's been an—accident—and Terry Campbell is—well—dead."

Sue gasped and Chris took her hand, but the date leaned forward, suddenly alert, and asked, "What type of accident?"

The chief squared his shoulders and said evenly, "She may have been murdered."

Chris went white and Sue asked incoherently, "What...why...I don't..."

"Look, I know you'd just like to be left alone now, and I sure wish I could do that, but I've got to get some facts from you, and ask some questions."

"Go ahead, Al," Chris said. "What do you need to know?"

"Full name of deceased?"

"Terry Campbell Townsend Weston O'Neill."

"Married?"

"Divorcing."

"Address?"

"223 Greenleaf Road," Sue said. "Indian Heights, Ohio. It's a suburb of Cleveland."

"Who'd be her closest relatives?"

"Her parents, Clarkson and Dorothy Campbell. They're out at their cottage. Wiley Point Road, Holcomb Harbor. And my folks."

"Who else? Brothers, sisters, kids?"

"No. No siblings, no children."

"Okay, now you." The chief turned to Terry's date. "Please identify yourself."

"Name is Dennis Wishon," he said in an uneducated but extremely assured voice. "I live in Cleveland."

"You have any IDs?"

"Yes," he said, but made no move to produce them.

"What's your occupation?"

"Businessman."

"What was your relationship to the deceased?"

"Friend."

The chief looked skeptical, and Wishon, just for a moment, looked amused.

"We'll discuss that later. Where were you during the last hour or two?"

"At the bar, mostly, and there's a room full of people who saw me."

The chief glanced at Chris, who nodded slightly.

"Drinking all night and you never left to go to the can?"

"Sure I did. So what?"

"And you made a phone call," I said. "I saw you at the phone booth."

"Oh, yeah, a phone call. Big deal."

"Why'd you come here?"

"To do a favor for a friend. Terry thought I'd be a good date."

"So you spent the night at the bar? Is that your idea of being a good date?"

He shrugged. "She was having fun without me, and I'm not the best dancer around. Hey, am I under suspicion of something?"

"So far, only of not leveling with me. What if I told you a quick look at the bed, and the body, leads us to believe she was with a man in the room, in bed, while you were drinking?"

I was interested to see that while the Campbells both looked pained, neither of them looked surprised.

"That so?" Wishon said. "I'd say it wasn't in the greatest taste to screw someone else when she was here with me, but, hey, like I said, we were just friends. I'm not saying I wouldn't lose my head if she was my main woman, but with us, it was strictly no-strings. A few drinks, a few laughs. Yeah, sometimes the laughs were in bed, but look," he turned to the others, "I know she was family and she sure didn't deserve this, but I can't pretend I'm the heartbroken lover. She was a lot of fun, a great-looking lady, but," he shrugged, "that was it."

The chief said, "We might have more questions so keep in touch. Let us know where to reach you when you leave town."

"Due to ladies, I won't say what comes to mind for an answer to that," he said coolly. "I have a few days here, for some vacation, and then I'm back to my own life."

"We'll see about that. For now I'm done with you." He looked around. "I want to see that kid who brought Tony the message—hey, what time was this party due to break up?"

Sue said, "One o'clock."

"It's twelve-forty now." He ran his hands through his hair. "Tomorrow's soon enough. You know where I can get a list of everyone who was here?"

"Actually," Sue said, "from me. I was cochair."

"Good." The chief nodded. "Good. Just bring it down to me in the morning, would you?" He sighed again. "You folks spend the evening with her? If Wishon's story checks out, we'll have to find the man who was with her."

Tony and I looked at each other, and I saw, also, that Sue's expression became just a touch grimmer.

"I think we know who it was," Tony said. "At least, Kay and I do. I think we all do." Sue nodded slightly, as if giving him permission to go on.

"The guy was probably Richie McDowell. We heard them in the garden, talking about going to her room."

"Richie? That stupid, goddamn, stupid—" The chief broke off with a visible effort. "Sorry. Laurie's my goddaughter. I always thought he was...oh, hell. I've got to get this straight.'' He took a deep breath, trying to regain his self-control. "You heard them? Did you see them? And why the blazing hell didn't you say something before?''

"Because I don't know for sure that it was Richie,'' Tony responded angrily. "Because I'm not thinking clearly after half an hour locked in a room with a corpse I happen to be related to. Because I'm not too proud of being related to someone like Terry and didn't want to advertise her behavior...I don't know,'' he wound down. "I should have.''

"We saw them. We didn't see the man very well, but the voice and size and clothes seemed to be Richie's and—''

"It doesn't matter,'' Sue said soothingly. "Everyone in the room saw them glued together on the dance floor. Someone would have said something sooner or later.''

"The guy's a loser. I always knew it. Now I've got to question him and I'd like to spare Laurie if I can.''

"Maybe we can help,'' Sue offered. "Maybe I could get her involved in something while you talk to Richie.''

"I'd appreciate it if you could do it, Mrs. Campbell.''

"Give me a minute... Yes, I know how. Pictures. I'll tell her we need pictures of the old cheerleading squad, and I'll ask her to round them up.''

"Good. Do it. Harrington, go get Rich McDowell and for God's sake be discreet about it.''

After Sue and Chris left, the chief turned to the rest of us. "You can't be here while I question Rich. I should really have him down to the station, but I don't want Laurie to know any sooner than she has to. Wait in there." He jerked his thumb toward the door to an adjoining room. "Stay in hollering distance. I might actually need you to tell your stories in front of the idiot. Davis, you stay to take notes."

We all sat as far away from the doors as possible, trying to hear every word while looking as if we weren't even listening. At least I was.

Finally Wishon said, "Who are we kidding? We all know we want to hear." He found a seat near the door and I followed. Tony remained where he was, slouched in a chair, feet up on a table, staring moodily out the window.

"Al, what's going on?" Richie was saying. "Is there a problem at home? The kids—"

"Sit down, Rich. No problem at home. The problem's here. We've got tough news and we're keeping it under wraps for tonight. Terry Campbell whatever-her-name is dead."

I wished I could see their faces. I was sure the chief's pause just then was deliberate.

"Dead? Terry? *Dead?* But how? I just...I just danced with her..."

"So we heard. We'd like to know more about that."

"What...what do you mean? We danced. We're old friends and classmates. Laurie knew."

"Did she know anything else?" Even through the door I could hear the chief's barely controlled anger.

"Al, for God's sake, what are you talking about? Tell me what's going on."

"Okay, Richie, my boy, my godchild's husband. Terry was murdered, in her bed, and we know she'd been with a man. Now you don't *have* to tell us anything, but you'd just save us a lot of time and trouble if you would. We can prove it all anyway. We've got tests, you know."

"Murdered. My poor beautiful Terry. I can't take it in." His voice broke.

"Rich!"

"Yes, I was dancing with her tonight. So what?"

There was a long silence. Then the chief said, very, very calmly, "I've got two witnesses who heard you in the garden."

Then McDowell did begin to sob. "Oh, God," he said. "I was with Terry. It's true. Don't tell Laurie."

"You might have thought of that before."

"I did. I always thought about it. I didn't really love Terry. I love Laurie—but Terry was—Terry was my dream—ever since we were teenagers. I couldn't believe my luck when she started dating me. She was the first girl I ever slept with, and she was all woman even then, when Laurie was saying, 'Not till we're married.' We've been lovers all along, whenever she came back for a visit. I never wanted to hurt Laurie—Al, you've got to believe me—but I was weak. I prayed she would never find out, and she never did. I just couldn't let Terry go. Don't blame her," he said with pathetic gallantry. "She broke it off again and again, but I always begged her to take me back."

In our room, behind me, I heard Tony have a coughing fit.

"And tonight?" the chief asked.

"We went to her room. After, she asked me to order her a drink and then I just left. I felt so damn guilty, I sat in the garden awhile until I could face Laurie. After that I stuck real close to her, feeling like a louse. She doesn't have to know, does she? Please, Al!"

"That depends on whether or not you killed Terry."

"Killed her? Me? I was crazy about her. I would never hurt her."

"McDowell, I'm going to tell you something I've kept to myself for twenty-five years. You're an idiot. I thought so when Laurie began dating you and I sure as hell haven't seen any reason since then to change my mind. The only reason I'm not hauling you down to the station on suspicion is that I don't want to hurt Laurie if I don't have to. You'll have to come down tomorrow and make an official statement, anyway. For now, just sign these notes. Then go find your wife and so help me, if she hears a word of this from you, even if you're innocent, you're as good as dead. You reading me loud and clear? Now get your face in order and get it out of my sight!"

"Yes, sir."

We heard the door open and close, and assumed it was all right for us to come out.

"I may need to talk to you all later," the chief said wearily. "Give Harrington your local numbers and where you can be reached if you have to leave." He shook his head. "People are asking my men all kinds of questions. Some folks saw the ambulance and the police cars, too. Seems like I'll have to make an announcement after all. Some reunion." He turned to the young policeman. "Where the hell is Davis?"

"He went to find the manager, sir, and see about the messenger and any other employees who were around."

"Oh. Okay. Good." He turned back to us. "Go on home. There's no more to do tonight."

We met Chris and Sue in the hall as we were leaving.

"Kay," Sue said, "will you be all right tonight, staying here? Do you want to come to our place? We have plenty of room."

Chris added, "Seriously, Kay, you'd be welcome."

"No, no thanks, I'll be fine. I'm dead tired though— ouch. Poor word choice. I'm sorry. Oh, yes, my car is still at your house. I'll pick it up tomorrow."

"Fine. We'll see you then. Good night."

Tony walked me to my room.

"You're sure you'll be all right?"

I was getting exasperated. "You know, I've been in a few war zones. I think I can manage a Falls City Sheraton Inn."

"Oh, I know. Just didn't want anything to interfere with our sailing date."

"You mean this won't?" I asked, surprised.

"Not unless I'm under arrest by then," he said a little too lightly. "Anyway, my parents are away, so I can try to put off family duties for a few days. So we're on? I'll call in the late morning, okay?"

I nodded.

In quite a different voice, he said, "I'm glad I met you again, Kay," and kissed me lightly, somewhere between mouth and cheek, and was gone.

SEVEN

Sunday morning

I WAS STRUGGLING to breathe, gasping, choking. I tried to scream but strong hands around my throat cut off the sound. In the dark I thrashed about wildly trying to break free. I clawed at the fingers pressing, pressing down on my windpipe. I was losing consciousness, slipping, slipping, slipping down, when I forced myself to open my eyes—in a sun-flooded room, alone and safe. I lay still, slowly waking up to the realization that it was a dream.

I wasn't as tough about Terry as I thought. And I felt awful. Too much to drink and too little sleep.

A long hot shower and a pot of room-service coffee helped clear my head, and then I swung into action. I was staying and that meant taking care of details: canceling my flight reservation, extending my car rental and room, calling the office.

I looked over the meager contents of my suitcase and added: Buy some clothes. Get laundry done. That reminded me to look at my gown, still in a crumpled heap on the floor where, apparently, I had stepped out of it last night. One more item: Find a good dry cleaner.

I heard the maids in the hall and stepped out, taking the dress to show them.

"Can any of you tell me who is the best dry cleaner in town? This gown needs a lot of careful work."

"Oh, what a pretty dress!" one of them said. "Could this be yours? I found it right here in the hall and the color's right. I thought someone must have lost it at the party last night." She held out a hair ornament, a stiff bow of pale green ribbon, trimmed with flowers and sewed to a comb.

"No," I said, patting my short hair, "it does match, but I wouldn't have a place to put it. It looks familiar, though. I'll try to remember who might have been wearing it. Now about my dress? And I need to get some laundry done too."

"Oh, sure. They can arrange it all for you at the desk."

I quickly knocked off the other items on my list, except for shopping, and felt I had earned, and was now ready for, a large breakfast. I was hoping to find some of my former classmates in the dining room, but the only person there that I recognized was Dennis Wishon. That was fine with me. It was the perfect opportunity to ask some questions. I quickly filled a plate from the hotel's Famous Sunday Buffet Brunch and walked over to his table with my most ingratiating smile in place.

"May I join you?"

"There's an empty chair," he said unenthusiastically, "but I'm leaving right after this cup of coffee."

"A few minutes of company is better than none," I said pleasantly. "I hate eating alone in a hotel restaurant. Don't you?'' Actually, I relished the quiet and anonymity, and the chance to prepare myself for whatever the day might bring.

Wishon replied, with no change of expression, ''Don't mind it at all. Mostly, I prefer it.'' Before I could say anything else, he said, ''No point in talking about last night. There's nothing to say. Poor, stupid bitch. You're not a relative, are you?''

''No, I just happened to be there at the time. I don't think we were ever really introduced. My name is Kay Engels.''

He looked at me very carefully for a moment. ''You some kind of reporter?''

''Yes, I am. How did you know?''

''I knew I'd seen you before. You once did a story about an associate of mine.''

''I'm flattered that you remember,'' I said with a smile, my mind racing, trying to make a connection.

''Oh, he didn't like that story, not at all. It would be hard to forget your name, what with all the unprintable words he attached to it. Of course there was a lot of us who thought the story was dead-on. Probably that's what he didn't like about it.''

''Who was it?''

He gave me another thoughtful look before saying, ''I don't think I'd care to say. I'm not here to discuss my business life. I wouldn't recommend you prying into it either, just in case you're thinking about it.''

I made my face a perfect blank and told a half-lie in a perfectly calm voice. "I'm here on a personal visit, not business."

"Sure," he said. "Just thought I'd mention it. My business is entirely personal too, and I don't plan to let anyone interfere with it. Got that? Now, if you'll excuse me, I have a few matters to attend to."

I thought, I'll know who you are in twenty-four hours. You look like a man with a few secrets, but not for long. Not from me.

Our library at the magazine is huge, well-stocked, and staffed every day. I called and asked for a thorough search on Dennis Wishon, of Cleveland, occupation unknown, and fax the results please, ASAP. I added, for security, that they should black out his name.

There was one last item left on my list of tasks. I called for a cab to take me to the Campbells' house to get my car. It was still parked in the driveway, next to a navy blue BMW and behind a brown Saab Turbo.

Chris was in front, watering the lawn in cutoff jeans and faded sports shirt. He looked up as the cab approached, blue eyes squinting into the sun. I thought that age had not made him any less good looking, and was relieved that it was a totally dispassionate thought. I didn't feel even a trace of the old tremor.

He put down the hose and came toward me with a smile. Up close, I could see how exhausted he looked. I said, "How are things?"

"I don't know," he said, rubbing his head in a small boy's gesture. "It's been quite a night. Sue's with my aunt and uncle, Terry's parents, hand-holding. I was up most of the night, on the phone and so on."

"Does everyone in town know?"

"Seems like it. I finally switched the phone directly to the answering machine. It'll be on the news tonight and then all hell will really break loose." He shook his head. "I'm glad there's no local paper on Sundays.

"Hey, I'm keeping you out here standing in the sun. I'm sorry. Have you got a few minutes? Care to come in for a cool drink? I'd be grateful for the company."

"Yes, of course."

"What'll it be? Cold beer? Gin and tonic? Wine?"

"After last night, I think I'll stick to plain soda, thanks."

Head in the refrigerator, Chris said, "Lemonade, tonic, bitter lemon, iced tea, cola? I hope you don't mind if I do have a gin and tonic. I know it's early, but I could use one."

I chose iced tea, and we took our drinks into the airy, pastel family room off the kitchen.

"Let's not talk about Terry now," Chris said with a sigh. "I'd just like to forget for a while. We couldn't talk much last night. I was too busy hosting. Tell me about you."

"I'd rather hear about you," I said with a smile, honestly curious to see what kind of man he had become. "What's life like here for someone who really went away for college—Dartmouth, wasn't it?—and then came back.''

"It's good. It was fine to go away, meet people from all over and test myself and all that, but I belong here. You know, my great-great-grandparents were born here, and their parents were some of the first settlers. My folks live in a house my great-grandfather built in 1875. There's a place right here in this town labeled Chris Campbell, and it fits me just fine. I like banking, and I like it here, where it's a little personal. I went to Wharton for my MBA. I could have had a job on Wall Street or anywhere, and I chose this.''

"Sue says you're active in the community.''

"Oh, sure,'' he said, reddening slightly under his tan. "I've been given a lot. I feel like I ought to give some of it back, and just between you and me, it's a heck of a lot more rewarding than banking, anyway. But,'' he went on, pointing to a shelf of family portraits of Sue and children at various ages, and a bulletin board of snapshots, "that's where my life really begins and ends.''

I looked at Chris looking at the pictures of the boys in Little League uniforms, in Scout uniforms, in suit and tie for family portraits, and said, "They really mean a lot to you, don't they?''

"Everything, that's all. I might not put it like this to everyone,'' he said, "but somehow I feel you would understand. Funny, isn't it? When I haven't seen you in twenty years and you don't even have kids.'' He went on, "Without them, none of the rest would mean a thing. I'd have nothing and be no one."

I answered him matter of factly. "You felt like telling me because I know how to listen. It happens all the time. It's part of my work." I added quickly, "I'm not doing it on purpose with you, though. I'm being perfectly straight with you."

Chris frowned a little, hesitated, then finally said, "There's something I'd like to be straight about with you. You seemed to be very friendly with Tony last night. Be careful, Kay. He's not entirely... dependable." He saw my expression and said quickly, "I'm sorry. Maybe that was out of line. Please take it as coming from exhaustion and good intentions. No hard feelings?"

"Not at all," I said, with only partial honesty, "but look at the time! I have to run. Thanks for introducing me to your family."

"Thanks for the company," Chris said, taking my hand for a moment. "Let us see you before you go back to New York."

I left uncomfortable, wondering just what Chris meant and what the obvious ill-feeling between him and Tony was all about.

Anyway, I thought, irritably, it has nothing to do with me. I'm a big girl now and I've certainly been around enough to make my own judgments about men. I suppose I was willfully ignoring all the times my judgment had been dead wrong.

When I returned to the hotel there was a message waiting for me from Tony, asking me to call him.

"How is everything?"

"Could be better. I may have to ask for a rain check on that sailing date. Maybe not. I have some family responsibilities after all. Care to take a little ride into the country with me instead, and meet the best of my relatives?"

"Yes, that would be fine."

"I'll pick you up in fifteen minutes."

We drove out of the city on the interstate, heading north toward the Canadian border, but we soon left it for an old county road that meandered across farm-land and through small villages. We were going toward the lake, I thought, but I wasn't sure I remembered the geography of the county.

It was a bright summer Sunday. The green fields were dotted with black-and-white cows. The roads and the village streets were almost empty. The only people we saw were an occasional farmer on a tractor and some children playing with a dog in front of a village house. Twice I saw hawks circling high up in the sky. I sat back, letting the breeze from the open window ruffle my hair, looking around at a landscape filled with peace, abundance, and stability, where twenty years ago I would have seen only emptiness.

There was a nagging thought invading my peace. I opened my eyes and said suddenly, "Tony, what did you mean last night when you said, 'If I'm not arrested by tomorrow?'"

He looked embarrassed. "It was a poor attempt at a joke." He stopped for a moment, then went on, speaking carefully. "But Kay, hasn't it crossed your mind that I'm under suspicion, at least as much as several others?"

"Because you found her."

"Sure. I was there. I had the opportunity. No one knows if she was alive when I went to the room."

"But Tony—"

"Of course. There's no evidence and there won't be any, since I didn't do it. And no motive either. I disliked her a lot—me and half the people at the reunion—but even I don't think she deserved that. I think."

"Does the chief think you did it?"

"I don't know. I doubt it, but he had a lot of questions this morning and he said there'd be more. He remembers me from my wild youth. He was already a cop then. I've known him a couple of years as an adult, and we have an okay relationship. He's never brought up the old days, now that I've become respectable, but I know he's never forgotten them."

I turned to look at him, but I couldn't read his face. I asked, "Are you worried?"

"Not really." He grinned. "How does it feel to be on a date with a possible murder suspect?"

"Actually, you're not the first murder suspect I've ever known. So there!" But, I thought, I certainly never dated one. And how do I know you're telling the truth, anyway?

EIGHT

TONY STOPPED AT a gas station to make a phone call and returned, saying with a grin, "The person we have to see said to come after dinner, she's too busy canning tomatoes now. I should tell you that she's about seventy-six." He looked up at the sky. "It's a perfect day for sailing, and it's not that late. We're five minutes from my cottage. Suppose we get in a short sail now, and have dinner out here?"

"Sounds wonderful."

He looked critically at my high-heeled sandals, beige jersey pants, and beige-and-black cotton sweater, intended to be my traveling outfit. "Those shoes won't be safe on the boat. Better go barefoot and roll those pants up. I can loan you a windbreaker."

In a few minutes he turned up a dirt road and then we were at the river, driving up to a small house covered in weather-stained green shingles, with a big, glassed-in porch facing the river. I liked it.

"The place you spent your summers as a kid?"

"Oh, no," Tony said dryly. "That's thirty miles along the lake, down at the Harbor. It's a modest fifteen-room cottage on a private road, with an acre of land and all my relatives nearby. No, this is all mine. I have an apartment in town, of course, but this is home.

I'm having it winterized. It's the first place I could ever say was really mine. Come see."

"What about your place in New York?"

"My wife's choice. Her neighborhood, her style, her home."

We stood in a large wood-paneled room with a stone fireplace at one end. There was a small kitchen with a counter and stools, and a more spacious dining room beyond. A ladder led up to what I assumed was a sleeping loft. Large windows allowed us to look out over the porch to the wide river dotted with islands, all green fir and gray stone, and to the dock with a sailboat and a rowboat tied up to it.

"Here's where I sleep—" Tony was opening doors. "Bathroom—kids have the whole attic when they're here. What do you think?"

"I think it's perfect."

"The woman is a genius. Let's go. We're wasting what's left of a beautiful afternoon. Bring those shoes along, for dinner, and let's see—towels, jackets, sodas—we're set."

It was the end of a sparkling afternoon, with a smart breeze off the lake and enough sun left to keep us warm. Tony handled the trim little boat expertly and required little crewing from me. We sailed in and out of hundreds of small islands, avoiding the deep channels where the cargo boats traveled up from the Seaway. Most of the islands had summer homes on them, some just cabins, others quite magnificent. Island dwellers waved as we went past, and we waved back.

"Tony," I said, "this is heaven."

"Isn't it? This helped me get some sanity back when I came back here, and my kids love it. It's something I can give them that's special about being here."

"Tell me about your kids."

"I will, later. We're here."

We were approaching one of the islands. Tony brought the boat in easily and we tied up at a dock crowded with sailboats and motorboats of all sizes, from rowboats fitted with outboard motors to cabin cruisers. We walked up a small hill to the only building I could see, an old white house with a side porch.

"This is it. It only serves fishermen and boaters. In fact, there's no way to get here except by boat, and it only serves one meal but it's a perfect one."

And so it was. It was a crowded, informal restaurant, a small house, really, with tables covered in red-checked oilcloth set up in the living room, dining room, and porch. It was a pleasure to eat on the porch, surrounded by tall pines, watching the river and eventually, the blazing sunset over the darkening island. I enjoyed the chopped chicken livers on toast served as an appetizer, the fresh sweet corn on the cob and crunchy coleslaw, the perfect fried chicken and gravy, the fluffy biscuits and homemade pie. There was much talk back and forth among the tables about fishing conditions, weather, the state of the river. I enjoyed that too, and I enjoyed watching Tony join in, easily and enthusiastically, the ironic undertone completely gone from his voice.

When we left it was still the long summer twilight, with the light fading but not yet completely gone. Back in the boat I said, "You were going to tell me about your children."

"Yes. It was too noisy in there. I have two daughters. Peggy is ten, Catherine is seven. They're at camp for a month. This is the first time I haven't had them for most of the summer. They're great kids, completely different from each other but pretty good friends. They're not spoiled, at least not yet, in spite of the life they lead out there with their mother. I keep things here as simple as I can on purpose, and thank God, they seem to like it when they're here." He was silent for a while, then went on, "I know now how much I missed when they were small. I worked so many weekends, and they were already asleep so many nights when I came home. You know about that kind of life. You kid yourself that you're doing it all for them, and before you know it, you've missed whole years out of their lives. When they're here now I try to give them every minute I can. They have to go to day camp while I work, but I walk out at five every day if they're here. They change so fast, I never know who they'll be when they get off that plane, and I don't want to miss one minute more than I have to."

He was quiet for a moment, busy with the boat. Then his voice, completely unguarded, floated back to me through the darkness. "I miss them so much."

A moment later we were docking. We got back into the car and drove away from the river, and in ten minutes or so Tony was turning onto a dirt road with fields on either side. He drove perhaps half a mile, stopped in front of a white farmhouse with gingerbread trim on the porch and steep gables, bounded up the steps, and knocked loudly on the screen door. The front door behind it was open and he shouted, "Hey, Maggie, are you home? I've brought you a visitor."

A tall woman with a fluff of white hair came to the door and said in a loud, deep voice, "Tony, I didn't hear you at first. What a nice surprise. Come in, come in, and who's your friend?"

"Maggie, this is Kay Engels, up from New York. Kay, this is Maggie Prestwick, my aunt and the only one of my relatives I can stand."

"Come into my parlor and tell me about this reunion, Tony. I thought you'd still be in town tonight."

The parlor was quite a surprise. I was expecting a cozy farmhouse room with a hodgepodge of Victorian furniture, perhaps adorned with crocheted antimacassars. Instead, I found a spacious modern room with a skylight and Scandinavian furniture. Indian blankets hung on the walls and Indian pottery and baskets rested on the shelves, tables, and floor.

"You like my room," Maggie said with a grin. "I can see it in your face. We bought most of that furniture in Europe, way back in the early sixties, when Harry had a Fulbright. God, what a long time ago that was! Tony, pass me those cigarettes, will you? Can I offer you a drink, or some coffee?"

"Nothing for me. Kay?" I shook my head and he turned back to Maggie. "Hey, you. I thought you were going to give up cigarettes?"

"Puh-leeze! I gave up men when Harry died, and I had to give up booze and sweets when I went on insulin a few years ago. This is about the only vice I can still enjoy." She inhaled deeply and exhaled toward the ceiling. "I can still blow smoke rings, too."

Tony grinned like a boy. "Do you remember how you made friends with me, that first time you came back from Arizona, by blowing smoke rings? You promised to teach me as soon as I could stand smoking."

"I certainly do remember. We've been friends ever since." She turned to me and confided, "That's because we're the family outcasts. I never could stand most of my relatives and Tony here spent most of his youth trying to antagonize all of them. Couldn't blame him, though he might have chosen his methods more wisely. Anyway we took each other just as we were, and no one else understood either of us. Right, Tony?"

"That's true. Maggie was the big family rebel in her day. Instead of coming home after college and marrying appropriately, she went off out west to work with the Indians."

"That explains—" I gestured around the room.

"Partly, partly. Each of these things has its own story. Yes, I went out to the Indians—Native Americans, I should say now, but I forget sometimes—originally as a teacher at a mission school, but after a while

I saw I had as much to learn as to teach, so I stayed, teaching and learning, studying, nursing, doing some political work. I was there about twenty years. My, it seemed to go so fast.

"Then," she said with another grin, "I up and surprised everyone, and no one more than myself, by getting married when I'd already been an old maid for years and years. Married to a college professor from right here in the North Country, too. I met him out there when he was on a sabbatical. He convinced me there were Indians back here, too, and so there were, scattered on small reservations. I got involved with some of the New York State tribes. In fact, there's a reservation just a few miles from here.

"We always spent a lot of time in this house," she went on slowly, "and we moved here full-time when Harry retired. This farm's been in my family since 1818, stolen from those same tribes, of course. That's why I'm planning to give it back to them in my will."

"I read about you in the paper yesterday."

"I'm sure they got it all wrong," she said tartly. "They did last time they wrote about it. I ran into a little snag with the tax people, but I think we're going to work it out. I've got a meeting with them Tuesday."

She looked at Tony, who had been wandering restlessly about the room, looking at this and that. "Tony, stop fidgeting. You've got something on your mind. I can tell. You didn't come out here just to be bored by the story of my life. Spit it out."

"Okay, Maggie," he said, sitting down and taking her hands in his. "I've got some news. It's family news and not good." He took a deep breath and looked at me. "I'm finding it hard to say."

He started again. "Maggie, there's been a death in the family and it's a particularly ugly one. Terry Campbell is dead. She was murdered last night." He told her about the events of the previous night.

"Murdered? My God. Her poor parents... They dote on her so... always did. Oh, Tony, give me another cigarette." She was silent for a moment, smoking. Then she said something surprising. "So someone finally did her in. I've been tempted to myself, and more than once. She was a poisonous child, flouncy and spoiled and a liar, too. Age did not improve her. Who do you suppose did it? One of her ex-husbands? I'm sure she had it coming."

"Maggie," Tony said, trying not to laugh, "that's the most immoral thing I've ever heard you say. You're supposed to be shocked, at least."

"Oh, fiddle, Tony, don't bore me with that nonsense. What's the good of being my age if I can't say what I think, at least to you? Kay isn't shocked. Are you, Kay? Don't worry. I'll go to the funeral and say all the right things. After all, she was my niece, even if I do think her father and my other brothers are pompous, boring, self-satisfied jackasses. God, I must have loved Harry to let him bring me within a thousand miles of my family! Sorry. I'm wandering. What I meant to say was just that here with you, I'll say whatever I damn well please.

"Well, well. Poor Terry after all. Stupid child never to have married for love. It might have saved her, but then, she was probably too selfish to love anyone. That's why she was so scared of getting old, you know. Even I could see it. Had to flirt with every man she saw, just to prove she could still get them. Tony!" she barked. "Do you remember that family party where she was making eyes at someone's boyfriend, and him only about eighteen?"

"Sounds right, but I must have missed that one. Unfortunately."

"Oh, yes, you were still in New York. It was Linda's wedding and little Rosemary brought her boyfriend. Damn near ran off with Terry by the end of the reception! Rosemary's dad was ready to kill her then and there. Well, well, a murder in the family. That's a first, I guess, or at least the first for sure. My mother always had some suspicions about Great-Uncle Joseph's first wife." She yawned. "I think you're keeping me up past my bedtime. I was milking cows at dawn, and I usually turn in to rest about this time. Go on home now, and come visit again. I'll tell you some stories about my Indian things, Kay." She winked. "It'll be nice to have a fresh audience."

"I will," I said, "gladly, if you wouldn't mind my writing them down and putting them in my story. I'm a reporter, and I'm supposed to be doing a story about the reunion, murder and all."

"I'd be flattered. If I could have done it myself, I'd have finished my Ph.D. in anthropology years ago. Harry was always after me to do it, but after he died—" She shrugged. "Come kiss me good-bye, Tony. I'm not too old to enjoy it."

We walked down the steps with Tony smiling and shaking his head. "I never thought she'd take it like that. What a woman."

"Tony, she's terrific."

"Oh, yes. I think she really saved my life more than once when I was a kid. Fear of having her think I was an idiot kept me from going that one step too far—and I went pretty far."

"If I could be like that at her age—"

"Her age? She's got more sense and brains and sheer gumption than most people half her age. More than the rest of my family put together, anyway."

"More than Terry ever had, it seems. Do you know when the funeral is?"

"No. A couple of days, I guess. Are you planning to stick around?"

"Yes. I'm going to write a story about the whole thing. I'll be here as long as I need to be to do it. Oh, damn!" I stopped short. "I have to cancel a date in New York on Thursday. I forgot all about it. And someone was planning to pick me up at the airport today. I forgot that, too. I'll have to call tonight and be very apologetic."

"Does it bother you much?" he asked in an odd voice.

"Forgetting? Or apologizing? Both. I don't like being stupid, and I *hate* admitting it."

"No, I meant canceling your date."

I shrugged and said, "It's part of the job."

"And here I thought it was my sailboat and my style on the dance floor that kept you here!"

I had to smile. "Maybe it helped. Just a bit, mind you."

We were quiet going back to town, strangely contented with our day together, perhaps deliberately trying to ignore for a few hours the ugly event of last night. At least I felt that way, and I thought Tony did too. When he said good night, he added, "Thanks, Kay. It was a good day, wasn't it? In spite of everything. I can't even feel guilty about enjoying it so much." Neither could I.

There was a package waiting for me at the hotel desk, five faxed pages from my office. The cover note was from one of the librarians, a friend of mine. It said, "Kay, you're in luck. It's not much, but, as Spencer Tracy once said in another context, 'what there is, is cherce.' Wish I could see your face when you read it."

There were computer printouts of three stories, from a newspaper and two magazines, with a starred blank spot in each story where Wishon's name had appeared.

No wonder he didn't want to talk to me! I thought. When I go to interview the chief tomorrow, he should roll out the red carpet for this. It's worth a week of charming smiles.

NINE

"YES, HOWARD, I *know* the murder makes a more gripping story. I *know* gripping stories sell magazines. No, Howard, I won't get sidetracked. Yes, I'll keep you posted. Of course I will. Yes, I know I have a new assignment coming up. Yes, I'll be back in time to prepare for it. But I can stay on this until then? Of course, I'll keep expenses within reason."

I was talking to my editor. He was excited by what I told him about the reunion, but decidedly not excited about my idea that I would like to do something in-depth on the changing life in small towns. He was unimpressed by my argument that in the long run it was probably a far more significant topic.

"It's ho-hum," he said. "Stick to the hot stuff."

I didn't say it to him, but I thought that there are no ho-hum stories, only ho-hum reporters. I would do the story anyway, and make him eat his words—on sixteen pound bond, too.

Just following the murder would mean several days, perhaps weeks, in Falls City. I was surprised at how little that bothered me. There was so much more I wanted to know about the town, the ways it had changed and the ways it hadn't; about my former classmates and what life had done to them; how they had grown and how they hadn't. I checked off some names in the reunion book, people whose briefly told stories had intrigued me on Saturday night.

Then I took a deep breath and guiltily called Jeremy, the younger friend from work who was getting a little too persistent in his desire to upgrade from friend to lover. I had to apologize for not letting him know I would not be on the flight he had insisted on meeting yesterday, and for ignoring the pile of messages I found when Tony dropped me at the hotel. Well, I thought with considerable irritation, who asked you to meet my flight anyway? When I told him about the murder and explained how it had driven everything else out of my mind he was understanding. Too understanding. He missed me, and was worried, and offered to come up for a few days to keep me company. He seemed hurt when I turned him down, even though I did it as gently as possible. I would have to do something about him, and soon.

My next call was to Peter, the longtime on-and-off man in my life. He's a real New York man-about-town: a successful advertising executive, a great date, a great lover, and prone to a fast fade at the least hint of any emotional claim. He was just what I thought I wanted.

He greeted me cheerfully. "Hi, babe. What are you doing still up there in the boondocks? How are you surviving?"

"Peter—"

"I know, I know, it isn't really the end of the world. I've been in the country once or twice myself, you know."

"Your idea of the country is the Hamptons. You know nothing about it."

"Touchy. I knew you couldn't last long in a place where there are no bagels."

"Peter," I said in my most businesslike voice, "I'm working, and I called for a reason."

"Let me guess," he said in a suddenly very quiet voice. "You're canceling our date for the gala on Thursday."

"How did you know? Oh, Peter, I am sorry—and I was looking forward to it, too."

"And so you should be. Any Easthampton Museum benefit is the social event of the summer, but this one is going to be the best yet. Not to mention what a great table I put together. Not to mention two wonderful days at the Eddystone Inn with me. It's a mistake, you know. Are you sure you can't make it?" For one surprising moment I thought he sounded genuinely disappointed.

"I just can't. There's an incredible story here, there was actually a murder at the reunion, and I can't pass up a story like that. You won't have any trouble getting another date. I really hate to do this."

"I knew it. I heard it in your voice. I've known you long enough to recognize that thrill of the chase sound. So, okay, make it a great story, and when you read about the dance in the *Times*, eat your heart out," he said more cheerfully. "Give me a call when you get back."

I thought he took it awfully well. It was almost insulting. Yet even as I thought it, I knew I didn't care about missing a glittering social event, and I didn't miss Peter either.

My next job was to tackle the chief of police. With the package from my office in hand, I could hardly wait. As I walked through the hotel lobby I noticed the very young desk clerk looking at a physical-fitness magazine.

"Would you know of any place in town where I could take an exercise class?" I asked.

The girl looked up with an enthusiastic smile. "Oh, sure. Of course there's swimming here. And I run about ten miles every day in Perkins Park. Those paths up and down the hills are a terrific workout. I feel great after that! I'd be happy to show you the best route."

I shuddered. "It takes too much willpower to get out there and run. My body may need exercise—in fact, it's screaming for it right now—but the rest of me hates it. I'd never do it without a teacher cracking the whip."

"Oh." The girl looked disappointed. She had not found a fellow enthusiast after all. "There's a good workout at the Y, Tuesdays and Thursdays. A gym teacher from the high school teaches it, Laurie McDowell."

"Perfect," I said, thinking it might also be the ideal chance to talk to Laurie. As I turned to leave the desk phone rang, and I heard the girl say, "Mr. Wishon doesn't seem to be in his room. Would you care to leave a message?" I turned back casually, as if I had just remembered to ask one more question. No one watching would have known it, but my entire attention was locked on the brief conversation.

There was a pause, then the girl said, "Yes, sir, I'll be sure he gets it. Yes, I understand it's confidential."

I never moved. Even my eyes would have seemed to be looking aimlessly at the clock on the wall, but I was reading upside down as the girl wrote, "Package arriving promptly at 4 P.M. today."

After the girl put the note in Wishon's box I asked for unneeded directions to cover my lingering and headed for the police station.

When I explained to the young man at the front desk that I had information about the murder, he promptly disappeared into the back and returned right away to show me into the chief's office.

"Good morning, Chief LaForge," I said cheerfully, extending my hand. "We met Saturday night. I'm Kay Engels."

He looked up without enthusiasm, and did not get up or shake my hand. "Have a seat. So you're the reporter. I didn't know that the other night."

"How did you find out?"

"I heard. If I'd've known, I wouldn't of let you hang around. I suppose you're planning to write about this mess?" he asked gloomily.

"Yes, of course. It's my job."

"It's *my* job to find out who killed that woman. Don't get in my way." He looked as if he meant it. "I don't need a smart-ass out-of-town reporter added to the local ones breathing down my neck and second-guessing me in print on top of all the other problems with this case."

He leaned back in his old-fashioned heavy wooden office chair and looked at me shrewdly. "Look at you, sitting there in your clothes that you didn't get at any J. C. Penney and your haircut from some la-di-da place that wasn't Myrtle's Cut 'n Curl, sitting here in my grubby hick-town police office. You don't belong here. Why don't you just go home?"

"But I do belong here," I said firmly. "I belong here more than most of the places I'm in. I've been in police stations on three continents, and at least half of them were painted this exact shade of government-issue green. They had windows like yours, too, washed once a decade. You've probably got the same lousy coffee all the others had, too." For a second I thought he was about to smile. "Chief, I've followed lots of police officers on lots of stories, and I certainly don't intend to be a nuisance. I might even be able to help. Look at this." I handed him the printouts.

His expression never changed, but his eyes lit up as he read. "Where'd you get this?"

"A librarian at my magazine found it for me. The embarrassing thing is that I wrote one of these stories myself."

"I see. So he's a 'reputed Ohio affiliate of Chicago gangland boss, "Crazy Horse" Harry.' Damn it," he said, slapping the desk and grinning, "I knew something wasn't right about him!"

"Look at the other two," I said, trying not to sound triumphant.

"'Closely questioned in the death of cocktail waitress, his frequent companion.' So she broke it off and turned up dead. Looks like they never proved anything. Never even made an arrest."

He added quickly, in a matter-of-fact tone, "Of course we would have found this information on our own."

"Of course," I agreed promptly, "but maybe I saved you some time?"

"Maybe. There isn't that much here. It's all interesting, I admit, but it doesn't even prove much about my case. We also know that the night of the murder he made a lot of phone calls from the lobby, not just one. The desk clerk told us. They were all to the same number, another pay phone. Cleveland. He only connected once. Makes me wonder...well, I don't know. What was so all-fired important?

"Still not one bit of this adds up to a damn thing, not even this stuff you're so excited about."

I could see that he wasn't going to give me an inch. I resolved to try one more time. I said casually, "I had a curious conversation with him yesterday morning. I ran into him in the hotel dining room. For someone who's supposed to be just on vacation—and does this seem like a likely place for that anyway?—he seemed in a hurry, as if he had business of his own. I wonder if Terry was actually a cover-up and he's really here on business."

"That sure would be worth knowing. Of course maybe he *is* on vacation. Maybe he likes muskie fishing better than, say, gambling in Atlantic City. Still, I'll have someone watching him. I hope I've got a couple of guys who can do it without being too noticeable," he said without much confidence. "Most of what they know about shadowing they probably learned watching *Miami Vice*." He tapped my papers. "At least now we know he's a wrong one. I don't have much experience with pro killers, but this didn't look like what I'd expect."

"On the other hand, if it was a crime of passion—?" I suggested.

"All right, all right," LaForge said gruffly, "you've got me talking, and yes, you've been some help. Now what do you really want?"

"A story, of course. For that, I need to be able to talk to you, find out what progress you're making, where you think it's going, maybe talk to your men, too." As he frowned, I went on quickly, "Remember, I'm not a newspaper reporter, under the gun of a daily deadline. I may not even write anything until it's all over, but I need to be able to follow it step by step to do a good story at the end."

"You won't write anything I haven't okayed?"

"You must know I can't promise that. But I can promise nothing will be written about the investigation for a while in any case. There isn't enough to make a story yet."

"All right," he said. "You can ask me questions sometimes—not every day—and I'll tell my men they can talk to you. You know," he said slowly, apparently thinking out loud, "maybe you can help us."

"How?"

"Keep an eye on Wishon. His room is next to yours now—we had to move him out of Terry's. Don't do police work for us. Just keep your eyes and ears open and let us know if you see anything, anything at all."

"I can tell you something right now, for whatever it's worth. He's expecting a package today at four. I overheard the desk taking a message. *Now* do I get to ask my questions?"

He made a note of what I had told him, and said, "Oh, all right. Don't take too long."

"Is Wishon your prime suspect?"

"Don't have one. We're looking into all the possibilities."

"And who would the others be?"

"Can't say now."

"Has there been any progress so far? I know it's early."

"Can't say anything about that either."

"Do you have the medical examiner's report yet?"

"No."

I threw down my pencil in exasperation. "Chief LaForge, you're not keeping your part of the bargain! I *did* bring you something useful, and you are *not* answering questions. I'd hate to have to start sneaking around behind your back to get some answers, and I don't suppose you'd like me to write, 'Official sources refuse to discuss progress of the case. Could that be because there isn't any?'"

For the first time that morning, the chief cracked a grudging smile. "Oh, so you're getting tough, are you? No, no, don't get mad. I admire that. Okay. The truth is, we really don't have any news yet. All we've found so far is that she—the deceased— ordered a drink delivered from the bar at about midnight. Or someone ordered one from her room. We got that from the bar records.

"That probably clears McDowell, by the way. The time is on the bill—it records automatically somehow—and he was out there in full view of the whole party, dancing with his wife, at that time."

"Could he have faked it somehow?"

He gave me a look of total disbelief. "Does he strike you as swift enough to set up an alibi?"

"Have you talked to the waiter who brought the drink?"

He shook his head. "We'd sure like to, but— wouldn't you know?—he left on vacation right after his shift. Camping. Up in the woods. No one knows just where he is, but we'll find him. I've got a whole list of questions for him."

"Any physical evidence?"

"We don't have all the results yet. We took prints, but they won't do us much good. Tony's will be all over the place, Richie's, Wishon's. The maids. Terry's own. Everybody and his brother. A big mess of nothing."

I said with a little smile, "Maybe you should look for whose prints aren't there."

"Very funny." He didn't appreciate my mild joke.

"And that's really it until you have the ME's report?"

"Yes, ma'am, that's really it." I rose and the chief walked me to the door. I had a feeling it was more from a desire to make sure I left than courtesy. By way of good-bye he said, "I know I'll be hearing from you."

When I left the police station I decided there wasn't much more I could do for my official assignment that day and that I could please myself by taking a long walk around town, getting reacquainted with this place I had not given ten minutes' thought to since I left. Besides, I was still annoyed at Howard, who thought selling magazines was more important than telling an interesting story. The hell with my assignment.

I looked at everything, eavesdropped shamelessly, and talked to anyone who would talk to me: the aging factory retirees sitting on the benches around the fountain in Central Square Park, enjoying the sun and arguing among themselves without heat about the old days; the serious, friendly volunteers at the Women's Center, who shared coffee and the local statistics on family violence; the lively group rehearsing a play at the experimental theater in a dark church basement. I noted that the county historical society was still housed in the same wonderfully spooky, turreted Victorian mansion I remembered; that the gleaming white marble library had a shiny new wing and an impressive collection; that my former elementary school was now a Christian Fellowship Academy. I made an appointment to interview the principal, who was anxious to talk about his mission, and another with the teachers at the Head Start Center, in what used to be the town's largest hardware store, who talked passionately about their quite different one. Several people mentioned the impending expansion of Fort Oake, and I made a note to introduce myself at the newspaper and arrange to talk to the military reporter. I was surprised at how much there was to learn, and thought fleetingly, with a grin, of Peter.

I had a sandwich for a late lunch in a shabby, darkly tiled, mirrored restaurant that seemed to have been preserved intact from about 1909. In New York, it would have been hung with ferns and promoted as authentic turn-of-the-century. Here it was just a pleasant old place with a badly typed menu and a single elderly, tired-looking waitress. She surprised me with a wink when I ordered a beer to go with my sandwich.

I even managed a blitzkrieg shopping trip to augment my two-day wardrobe. I found a black twill skirt, a black-and-white striped cotton shirt, and a black-and-tan print T-shirt to coordinate with my travel clothes. I added white pants, blue jeans, and a go-with-everything off-white cotton sweater, and then remembered I'd need a dress for the funeral. A black jersey sundress would do for going out and, covered by the short wrap jacket I'd worn on the plane, would be presentable for a funeral, too. I threw in some extra underwear, and then, as I was leaving, realized that the only day shoes I had were the two-inch-heeled black sandals I was standing in. I added a pair of cheap canvas flats and took out my credit card, wondering how much of this I could persuade my boss to let me expense.

Later, walking around, I passed a store full of colorful sportswear and remembered that I had packed a bathing suit, blue shorts, and a tropical shirt for possible poolside use at the hotel, and those were all the real summer sports clothes I had. I took what I could find in my size in the store—two pairs of shorts and a T-shirt printed in multi-colored stars—and knew I could now survive for a week or so.

I returned to my room after lunch tired but excited, as I always was when I was working. I was anxious to get my notes and impressions from the afternoon into my laptop computer while they were still fresh. But before I had accomplished much my concentration was destroyed by the sound of a door slamming so loudly it had to be the next room, where Wishon was now staying. I waited until I heard his footsteps go past and then opened my door a crack. Yes, it was definitely him. And he had the look of a man in a hurry.

TEN

WHERE COULD HE be going now, if he was expecting an important package in just a few hours? Well, the chief had that covered. His men would be watching. I was more interested in getting my impressions down quickly, in clear, punchy phrases.

I stepped over to my window just in time to see him get into his car, leaving the parking lot, and drive across the road to a gas station.

I was trying to think fast. Was he leaving? Gassing up for a trip? That was peculiar. Where are the police who should be watching him? LaForge said he would be shadowed. Should I call LaForge? Was there *time* to call him? I watched him move up the line at the pump. Damn it, I thought, I want to know what's going on, and LaForge won't tell me anyway.

I grabbed my purse, ran out to my car, and was at the parking-lot exit just as Wishon pulled up to the pump. I wondered if he would know me, but decided that the rented car was too ordinary to notice. As an extra precaution I put on my sunglasses and took a scarf from my purse. Folded into a triangle and arranged bandanna-style, knotted at the nape of my neck and pulled low on my forehead, it hid my shiny black hair and completely changed my appearance. I slid down in the car a bit to disguise my height and eased my car smoothly into traffic as Wishon left the station. I followed as he circled partway around Public Square, drove toward the edge of town, and got onto the interstate, heading north.

He drove carefully, fast but not fast enough to get stopped for speeding, and I kept up with him, always a few cars behind and never in the same lane. Traffic was so thin that I felt uncomfortably conspicuous, but I reminded myself that this was the main highway, after all. He couldn't possibly assume he was being followed here just because there was another car going the same way. I hoped he would stay on the highway and made up my mind that if he left it for any of the more isolated roads, I could no longer follow him safely. I would quit then and call the Falls City police.

He did not leave the highway at all. To my surprise, he continued all the way to the river and went over the first enormous span of the great bridge that crosses the Thousand Islands.

At this point I really wondered what the hell I had gotten myself into. He was going over to Canada, and I couldn't imagine why.

I held back as he approached the toll booth, letting other cars get between us in the line. I knew I couldn't lose him on the bridge.

The panorama of the river below was spectacularly beautiful, but my attention had to be focused forward, on the black sedan just ahead. We'd be reaching the border soon. As I followed the car across the first large island to the bridge's second span, I was trying to remember exactly what would happen at the border. We went across a short stone bridge over an inlet between two islands, with a U.S. flag at one end and a Canadian flag at the other. That was it. I was in Canada now and I managed to be just a car behind Wishon at Canadian immigration. I couldn't hear what Wishon was saying, but from the officer's gestures he seemed to be giving directions. He pointed left—west—and I realized with relief that I knew what the first big town in that direction would be. It was my turn.

"Good afternoon, ma'am. Where were you born?"

"Falls City, New York."

"And what is your destination today?"

"Kingston."

"Purpose?"

"Sightseeing."

"And how long do you plan to stay?"

"Just the afternoon, or the evening at most," I said, hoping it was true. If it would be more than that, I was turning right around.

"Bringing any liquor or tobacco? No? Very good. Enjoy your visit." He recorded my license plate and waved me on.

Amazing that it could be so simple. I'd forgotten that there were borders without passports, visas, and armed guards.

Wishon crossed over to the Canadian mainland and got directly onto 401, the main east-west highway. That told me nothing—our destination could be as near as

Kingston or as far as Vancouver. Wishon left the highway at the first town, though, a small place with an
Indian name and, judging by the enormous number of
motels, a substantial tourist business.

He wove in and out of traffic on the main street,
hesitating at a few intersections as though he were trying to see the names of streets. Then he made a right
turn so abruptly that I went sailing right on by and had
to turn around and come back, hoping I hadn't lost
him. He was just going around the next corner onto a
quiet street, and I wasn't sure I should continue. I
thought I would just see where he was going and then
drive past the intersection so I wouldn't be right behind him.

We were at the railroad station. I stopped on the
street as far from Wishon as I could get and still see
him from the parking lot. There were other cars in the
lot, a train was just coming in, and, yes, it was exactly
four o'clock. So the package was coming by train. Very
curious.

Wishon did not make a move to meet anyone on the
platform. As people started to come out of the station
and go toward waiting cars, I watched, waited to see
who would come out of the station and go to him. No
one did. Instead, a car pulled up next to his. It was a
late model, big, gray, comfortable, anonymous. In the
confusion of the arriving passengers and departing cars
I could easily have missed it. I'm sure no one else even
noticed it.

Wishon jumped out and went to talk to the driver. I could see two burly men in bright sports shirts in the front and someone else, much smaller, in dark clothes, in the back.

The second car left the parking lot, following Wishon, and I followed, a long, cautious way back. We left town the same way we had come in, going back toward the bridge. I knew I had been doing something dumb, right from the beginning, by following Wishon, and as soon as possible I merged gratefully into the heavy traffic on the highway.

Much too soon, both cars made a quick turn into a side road that led off into the trees. I stopped there, dying to follow and debating with myself just exactly how stupid it would be. Before I could decide, there was a hand on my car door and a voice saying, "Move over, miss. You're coming with me." Before I could say, "I certainly am not," I saw the gun in his hand.

I moved over and let him drive me into the woods, to where Wishon and the other man were waiting with the two cars.

Wishon snatched off my scarf and sunglasses. "I thought it was you. Stupid bitch. Do you think we're playing *Moonlighting* here?" He turned to the others. "She's a reporter. What do we do now?"

"Oh shit, Dennie. It's just like you to screw up. How the hell did she get on to you?"

"Shut up. There was nothing I could do about it. I could do something now," he said matter-of-factly, glancing from his gun to the woods beyond. I knew then that I was in big trouble, and cursed myself for being an impulsive fool. I also knew that I had to try to be calm, to watch and listen very carefully, to be ready to use any opportunity I found.

"No!" It was a sharp command from the second car. An old man, a very old man, in a dark topcoat and felt hat, wearing sunglasses, sat inside. "No, I tell you. Keep your mind on our business here, which is to get me into the United States and home with the greatest possible discretion. Leave a body here and who knows how soon someone will be looking for us?"

Who could he be, this frail-looking old man with an accent, who was apparently being smuggled across the border? Old and frail he might be, but these thugs certainly snapped to attention when he spoke.

The three younger men all started speaking at once, until he said, "Stop. I want to know some things. How far are we from this private airport you have found, Dennis?"

"About an hour, tops."

"And we have our plane there, with the pilot, and all ready to go?"

"He was there even before I left. We can get right out of the car and into the plane."

He nodded. "So we need some time. That is all. What is down the road? Houses or trees?"

"Woods. It's the only side road between the town and the bridge with nothing on it. I checked. That's why I picked this spot to make the transfer."

"Very good." The old man looked directly at me and I felt I could almost name him. Almost but not quite, and I had a feeling that if I could I had better keep it to myself, or I would certainly be signing my death warrant.

"Young lady, you are a great nuisance. I have important business, very important business, in the United States, and you are in my way. I wouldn't mind killing you, except for the questions it might create. This is not deep woods. I can't take a chance on some picknicker or fisherman finding your body today, and we don't have time to bury you. So, I let you live.

"Also I can't take a chance on you telling someone before I reach my destination. So, a very simple plan." He smiled. "One of my boys will take you down this road, three, four miles, in your car, take your car keys, take your wallet. By the time you walk to the road and get a ride somewhere, with no money and no identification, we will be long gone. A neat plan, eh, boys?"

Wishon protested. "She's a reporter. She'll tell everything she's heard here."

The old man stared at me again. "If she's a *smart* reporter, she won't. We can find her again. Remember that. And if she does tell," he smiled again, "who will believe her? No one will even know who she is. And she knows no names, except Denny's; no places, except here. Where are we going? Where are we coming from? She doesn't know. Even this car—you arranged so it can't be traced?" One of the men nodded. "So let her tell." The old man shrugged. "What can she do to us?

By the time she gets to friends, it will be too late to make problems. Go on, Denny. You take her, since you are already old friends. Joe will follow to bring you back. Vinny and me, we wait here."

Wishon grabbed my arm, holding tight enough to hurt, and pushed me into the passenger seat. He drove over the dirt road slowly, one hand on the wheel, the other holding his gun pointed at me. I sat very still, hands clenched into fists, praying we wouldn't hit a bump that would jar his finger.

When we stopped, he took the keys from the ignition, slid out of the car, and started to heave them into the woods. Then he stopped, and said, looking at me, "Nope, better not take any chances. Can't have you finding them, can we? The old man doesn't like mistakes." He grinned and pocketed them. "Now maybe I'd better take your whole purse here. No, he said wallet, and besides, this is too damn big to hide or throw away. Fucking women and their bags. Okay, I'll let you keep your makeup."

He opened my wallet, flipped through the bills, driver's license, credit cards, press ID. "It's all here," he said, and pocketed the wallet, too. "So that's about it. It will be some time before you can get to where you can tell tales. Just to make it a little harder—" He swung suddenly, unexpectedly, and smacked me with a powerful fist right across my mouth. The pain was so intense I almost passed out, and I felt my mouth filling with blood.

As Wishon walked to the other car, he called over his shoulder to me, "Have a nice trip back."

ELEVEN

I SAT MOTIONLESS in the car for quite a while, desperately trying to get control of the pain and shock. I put my head on my knees to fight off fainting and nausea. As soon as I was able to I got out, leaning hard on the car for support, and spit out the blood that filled my mouth. I moved my tongue around my gums, gingerly feeling for loose teeth. They seemed to be all right, but I could feel my lips swelling.

I thought dimly that I would give anything, anything at all in my power, for a drink of water to rinse out my mouth. And ice.

I sat in the car again, head back, eyes closed for a few more minutes, until the edge of the pain receded a bit. Since that drink of water would not come to me, I would have to go to it.

I opened my purse, reached into a zippered inner compartment, and took out my extra car key and emergency money. Over the years, I've had my purse snatched on the streets of Naples, my passport stolen in a Yugoslavian hotel, and my wallet lifted in a posh Fifty-seventh Street boutique in Manhattan. I've locked the keys into the car twice and once had a car key fall off my key ring and disappear. Now I insist on an extra key whenever I rent a car, and carry extra cash hidden in my purse. If my mouth hadn't hurt so much, I would have laughed at Wishon.

At the bridge, I told my story to the immigration and customs officers. They were solicitous and helpful, providing me with an ice pack, aspirin, and antiseptic, but they certainly didn't believe me right away. I was told, quite sternly, that I could not leave unless and until one of them told me otherwise. While I was being questioned indoors I could just see through the window that one of them was searching my car. They listened to my story several times, kindly didn't tell me what an idiot I had been, and called Chief LaForge for confirmation. Their own records showed that Wishon had crossed the border about half an hour earlier, alone in the car. The other car hadn't crossed at all.

They went over my story one last time. One of them said, "There's a private airfield at Falls City Airport, and there's one here in the islands. Bill, call the city and I'll get Bay Air Field."

I kept the ice pack pressed to my mouth and tried to hear the conversation.

"Hi, Tim. It's Jack Wright over here at the bridge. Oh, sure, everything's fine, but we heard a peculiar story just now, and we need to get some information. Did you have any small planes take off in the last hour or so? Probably two passengers, a big guy of forty maybe, and a little old guy?...Did they? Where to?...What about the plane and the pilot?...and the car?...Okay. Thanks a lot."

He turned to me. "Just as you said, a guy who sounds like Wishon and an old man in a dark coat. Sure would like to know how they hid him in the car. Anyway, we lost them. They took off about twenty minutes ago. We're going to take a good look at the car. They left it there at the airport. Their logged destination is Newark, but who knows? Pilot and plane aren't local. Supposedly from Jersey, and that we can check.

"Miss Engels, we don't know what you stumbled onto, but it was certainly something. We'll certainly be following up, and we thank you for reporting it all, though it would've been better to do it a lot sooner."

I nodded painfully in agreement.

"Is there anything else we can do for you? Would you like an escort back to the city?"

For one disoriented moment I thought he meant back to New York, but then I realized the city he had in mind was Falls City.

"No, no thanks," I mumbled. "Aspirin helped. If you ever find out, will you let me know? I have a real personal interest in the end of this story."

"I can understand that! We will if we can, depending on any investigation we get into."

I drove back cautiously, one-handed, using the other to keep the ice pack pressed to my mouth. I ordered two bowls of soup from room service to make up for my missed lunch, and spent the rest of the afternoon on the dreary business of buying a new wallet, canceling my credit cards and arranging emergency replacements, and replacing my driver's license. Then I had a chocolate milkshake for supper and collapsed at 7:00 P.M. into a twelve-hour sleep.

During the night, again and again I seemed to pass through one of those surreal twilight states in which I was asleep but dreamed I woke up and got out of bed. Or perhaps I was awake and so disoriented I thought I was only dreaming. It seemed that I couldn't tell the difference. Perhaps it was only a single episode that lasted all night long.

In one of my waking moments I saw someone standing outside my window. I sat up to scream but a voice in my mind said gently, "No, no, you're really asleep now and this is dreaming. Drift deeper and he'll go away." I watched myself in my dream, falling down and down, into a deeper sleep, and the figure at the window was gone, and so was I.

Tuesday morning

I WAS AWAKENED early the next morning by the pain throbbing in my mouth and the ringing of the phone. There was a voice saying, "I'm watching you, Kay. I have my eye on you."

"What...? What... Who...?"

"You won't always get away." The voice disappeared with a click.

That woke me up fast. My first thought, and fear, was that it was Wishon. The voice was somehow familiar, but I couldn't be sure. If only I had been more awake, I thought, when the phone rang again. I leapt to answer it. It was LaForge.

"Get yourself over to my office right away," he said without even a hello. He hung up before I could respond.

I'm not sure that my physical condition would have allowed me to argue; anyway, I knew that I had to tell him how Wishon had slipped away, and I suspected I would never hear the end of that story without his co-operation.

I did the best I could with cold water, hot coffee, and makeup, and eventually reached a point where I felt my mind was semiclear, my body was semifunctioning, and my face looked seminormal.

Perhaps I was fooling myself about that last item.

LaForge's first words were, "That's one hell of a bruise. Bet it hurts like hell too, don't it?"

I nodded painfully. That smack on my jaw seemed to have affected my neck muscles too.

"Heard you had yourself a little adventure over to Canada yesterday. Now just what in the name of all that's holy did you think you were doing?"

I opened my mouth to respond, but he went right on, "I had men on the way over to the hotel. If you'd've called, they could've followed him right out of town. Maybe arrested the whole bunch of them."

"For what?"

"I don't know, damn it! Something! I wanted Wishon right here for more questioning. Who knows where he is now? I'm not sure I couldn't arrest you for obstruction of justice." He glared at me. I wasn't sure he couldn't arrest me either, so I just glared right back. He was much too angry to tell about my mysterious phone call right now.

"It was goddamn stupid, you know. You trying to be a police officer?"

I shook my head.

"I'd like to take you straight to the airport and put you on a plane, but I probably can't. You haven't really done anything that would let me do it. Legally, anyway. Let me tell you, though, if you do anything like this again, I'll *find* some way to do it, even if I have to make something up. Is that clear?"

I nodded.

"All right," he said, a little more calmly. "You've paid for it. And yes, probably he wasn't involved with the murder. At least, we've got no evidence to say he was. Looks like he was here for something else altogether. We're going to find him anyway. Not us, exactly. Justice Department, now, *and* Treasury. They both take care of the border and they do not like what they heard yesterday. You can be sure they will find him. It just burns me up to think about him laying low somewhere and laughing at all of us. Okay, you can go, but goddamnit, don't pull any more stunts."

"I'd like to know what yesterday was all about." I could talk, I found, but only with some difficulty.

"I bet you would. Bet you'd like to know who killed Terry Campbell too, wouldn't you?" He laughed at my startled expression. "Well, so would we! No, we don't know, not yet. The medical report didn't tell us a thing we didn't know: she was strangled, recently had sex, had a lot to drink. No news there. No news at all.''

"And yesterday?"

"Yesterday. Very interesting set of events. 'Course it's officially a federal matter now. I'm not really involved, except as Wishon was supposed to be sticking around here.''

He knew something, though. I could see it in his face. What would be my best approach?

"You'll know anyway, won't you? Because you know everything around here.''

"One of the officers you talked to is a hunting buddy of mine. They're looking into all Wishon's connections. When they know, I expect I can find out.''

Bingo! I tried to smile. It hurt. "And you know I'll hound you until you tell me, don't you? I've got a personal interest in this one.''

"Guess you do, completely due to your own stupidity. You know *that*, don't you? Well, go on, I've got work to do, and nothing else to tell you now.''

I left, not knowing where I wanted to go. My mind still felt as fuzzy and my body as sluggish as if I'd been hit with a tranquilizer along with a fist.

When the thought first occurred to me I winced, but I suspected, most unwillingly, that an exercise class might sweat me back to normal. This was one of the days that Laurie McDowell taught at the Y.

Twenty minutes later I was panting and sweating, moving to music on Laurie's sharp commands.

"One and two and stretch and relax. Down on the floor for deep breathing for a count of sixty."

Lying on the floor, I studied my former classmate. She still had the body of a teenager, trim and supple, her muscles moving with perfect smoothness under her skin. Leading the class through a routine that left me panting, she had never even broken a sweat. Now, while the gym floor was covered with limp, exhausted, leotarded bodies, she was winding down with a routine on the gymnastics apparatus.

I was impressed. As Laurie swung herself through somersaults, I thought that she was incredibly energetic and strong for any age. If I couldn't see her face, I might have thought she still looked exactly like the high-school cheerleader I remembered. But I could see her face, with its deeply shadowed eyes and a mouth dragged down at the corners by deep lines. Her blond hair looked bleached, not too expertly, and was pulled back in a neat bun that made her face seem even more drawn. The professionally enthusiastic smile she wore during routines never went past her lips, and during the breaks her natural expression was one of sadness. Despair even. No matter how she looked to a casual glance, the pretty girl on the football field was gone forever.

After class I caught up with Laurie as she was gathering up her gear. "I really enjoyed that workout," I said untruthfully, "and I wanted to thank you. I'm a visitor here. I don't know if you remember me, but we were in high school together. My name is Kay Engels."

"Oh, yes," Laurie replied distractedly. "I remember. I'm glad you enjoyed the class. Excuse me. I'm in a hurry now."

She was walking away even while she was talking, but I walked comfortably beside her. "I'm sorry to hear that. I was hoping we could talk over lunch. I'm writing a story about how the town has changed, and I'd be interested in talking to you about the fitness craze and so on."

"No, no, I don't have time. I have to be at the junior high in ten minutes." Laurie practically ran through a door marked Office—No Admittance, letting it close on her last words.

I continued to think about her on the way back to the hotel, still determined to talk to her, still picturing her as she had looked disappearing into the office, in her businesslike black leotard with an incongruous ruffle over the hips, broad shoulders, slim waist, blond bun. Something about that picture was nudging my memory. It floated, that something, just out of reach, and I couldn't seem to bring it into focus.

TWELVE

I ACTUALLY DID feel better after the class, and it was still only mid-morning. I found a phone, dialed the office of the local paper, identified myself, and asked to speak to the managing editor. I suspected, correctly, that my own work would get me a cordial response.

"Good morning, Miss Engels. This is Scott Benson. What can the *Falls City Record* do for you?"

"Hello, Mr. Benson. I'm actually here in Falls City right now. I came for the high-school reunion—I'm from Falls City originally—and I'm trying to do a piece on the reunion, the changing town, and so on. Now I know that your people will be following this murder very closely and I don't mean to step on your toes about that; it's just part of my story. I really want to look at the whole community, and I can see that Fort Oake is perhaps the big thing right now. I was wondering if I could talk to some of your people about it, for background."

"Return of the native, eh? I don't see why not. We won't get in each other's way; we're not looking for the same story. Could you come down to the *Record* office this morning? I have some free time now, I can fill you in on local doings and introduce you to our military reporter. How's that?''

It turned out to be a productive morning. I talked shop for a few minutes with Scott Benson, and then he turned me over to a very young, very intense woman named Trisha Urbino.

''Come on, Kay. Let's grab a cup of coffee,'' she said as she led the way to her desk. ''I'll tell you what you'd like to know, and,'' she lowered her voice, ''you can tell me how you made the leap from Falls City to the big world.''

In the bleak cafeteria, I said, ''I need some background. I know I could go read library files, but I hoped you wouldn't mind being a shortcut.''

''Sure. All the stories in the files are mine, anyway. Until last year Fort Oake was Camp Oake, with a tiny maintenance crew all winter, but in the summer it was a training camp for reservists on summer duty, thousands of guys here in two-week shifts.''

''I remember,'' I said. ''The ones my father called weekend warriors.''

''Exactly. In real life they were accountants, teachers, plumbers, whatever, from New York or Philly, mostly. They spent a lot of money while they were here, and really, even though no one liked them much, the big fear every time Congress talked military budget cuts was that they'd shut down the base altogether. Then last year there was a new military bill and—presto!— Camp Oake becomes Fort Oake, a permanent, full-time, year-round operation. If you remember the weather up here," she added drily, "you won't be surprised to learn that it's going to be the home of a new mountain division, you know, specializing in snow-country fighting."

"Such as the Russian steppes?"

"That was the original idea, I believe. Now, who knows? But the division is still setting up here, even as we speak."

"Who managed to pull that deal off?"

Trisha grinned. "Read my files. It would take too long to tell, unless that's all you want to hear about."

"Is there anything in it that makes a real story?"

"I don't think so," Trisha said carefully. "At least, no one knows for sure. I *think* it's just politics as usual."

"You mean, no worse than usual?"

"That's it . . . probably."

"I'll read and see what I pick up. In the meantime, what really interests me is what's changing here in Falls City. We're talking about how many soldiers and families moving in?"

"About thirty thousand. Maybe a bit more."

"In a county with only—how many people now?"

"Fifty-eight thousand in the last census."

"So we're talking about major impact. How do people feel about it? I'm going to ask my own questions too, but I'm wondering what your perspective is on it. Do they understand just how big a change it will be? And what are the army's plans?"

"Of course they understand! Most people are thrilled." She smiled at my look of surprise, and emphasized, "*Thrilled*. I mean it. Don't forget, this is basically a poor, rural county. Oh, there's definitely substantial money here, too, but unemployment of 12 to 15 percent is *normal* in this county. Oake itself is going to generate a lot of jobs, and there will be a lot of spillover, too. They just broke ground for a big new shopping mall, with restaurants, theaters, classy shops. That never would have happened before.

"So, when you ask if they know how things will change, my answer has to be, Does anyone ever know? I mean, sure, there's going to be a whole lot of soldiers, some of them steady career types with families who'll blend right in, and lots of them eighteen-year-olds on the loose for the very first time. Bar owners are ecstatic; parents of teenage girls are nervous, I guess. Don't forget, though, that lots of men, and now even some women, around here were in the service themselves. It's always been an okay way to get away for kids who couldn't go to college or whose parents didn't want them to."

"I did know that," I admitted with some embarrassment, "but I'd forgotten. When I was protesting army recruitment on campuses, when I was away at college, half the boys from my old street were in the service."

All Trisha's information had been delivered at high speed, with great authority. I was amused. I wondered if she was me, fourteen years ago. I suspected she was.

I asked a one-word question, guessing Trisha would understand immediately all it implied.

"Demographics?"

"Oh, yes, all those dark-skinned guys from the streets of the big, bad cities. Well, some people don't like it. There's been some talk about how the crime rate will go up, and once they're actually here, dating local girls, I expect there might be some problems, but again, all kinds of guys have been coming here in the summer so people are sort of used to it. Some patriotic types feel that wearing the uniform cancels out all other differences, and some are just happy to take the money they'll spend, and they don't care whose hand it comes from.

"I'll tell you who's really nervous, and that's not the people here in the city, it's the folks out in towns like Old Mills. That's a little blink-and-it's-gone village right next to the base. Things are always a little edgy, let's say, out there in the summer, and they just aren't too happy about a year-round invasion. And," she finished soberly, "we're talking about country boys with hunting rifles in their cars, and real young soldiers with access to guns."

"Where will they all live? There can't be that much housing on base."

"A good question," Trisha said thoughtfully. "Lots of people are asking it. The army's renovating some of the old barracks, but you're right. That doesn't come close to filling the need. They are either going to build more housing themselves or contract with civilian builders. No one knows who or where or even when. Defense hasn't decided a thing yet as far as anyone knows, or anyone, including me, has been able to find out.

"Of course everyone's looking for a rise in real estate values. Very nice if you're my neighbor, putting off the move to Florida one more year to sell his split-level to a nice officer with kids for about twice what he could get for it today. Not so nice for the girl who cuts my hair, who's engaged to a gas station attendant and can't find an apartment they can afford."

"Trisha, this has been great. Probably I should look at those files, too. Do you have letters to the editors in them? It would be useful, I think, to read what people are thinking in their own words."

"I've got every single one that's been written, including the ones that weren't published. There's only one guy who objects on ideological grounds. Says we shouldn't be supporting the military-industrial complex. We don't know who he is. He always signs them 'Child of the Sixties.'

"Come on back to my cubicle. I'll show you the files, maps, stats, the works. I've got to go out to Old Mills this afternoon anyway. Want to come along and meet a few people?"

"I would love to," I answered, "but I'll have to take a rain check. Let me take you to lunch one day, to say thanks for letting me pick your brains."

"Great! I'll pick yours about your career. Here are the files. I've got to run, but you can just leave them here. Call me anytime if I can answer more questions.''

I spent several hours with Trisha's files, feeling more at home in the newspaper office than I had anywhere else in town. As I read through them I saw that she was a first-rate reporter. The news items detailing the minutiae of putting the base into operation, the intelligent background pieces, the letters displaying a wide range of reaction, all helped me develop a sense of an entire county on the brink of enormous change, holding its collective breath, waiting for the impact to hit. I left the newspaper building thinking the topic deserved a whole separate chapter in the book I was beginning to believe I would actually write.

When I returned to my room late in the afternoon the phone was ringing and it was Tony, suggesting dinner. I would have just enough time for ten minutes with an ice pack, a quick shower, and application of some heavy-duty makeup. I loved the way the thin straps of my new dress looked on my tanned shoulders, and hoped my plain gold hoop earrings, the only ones I had with me except for my emeralds, would distract attention from my bruised face.

When I met Tony, he looked at me oddly. ''Did you have an accident?''

''Sort of.'' I wasn't anxious to tell him how stupid I'd been.

''Hmmm.'' He continued to look at me. ''I was going to suggest a steak house, but maybe you'd prefer spaghetti.''

"Oh, yes," I said, with real gratitude.

In the car Tony and I agreed not to talk about the murder over dinner, and mostly we succeeded. We talked as any two people would just getting to know each other on a second date, but perhaps a little more easily than if we had not been old acquaintances. We shared bits and pieces of our lives, comparing impressions of life in New York, discovering a common interest in archaeology, and telling little stories from our working lives. I noted with interest that I was far more worldly than Tony and that he didn't seem at all bothered by that. He took it for granted, and was neither intimidated nor challenged.

Finally I couldn't resist telling him of my first discovery about Wishon. He was gratifyingly excited.

"I should have known. Kay, he reminded me of someone, and now I know who. I had dinner with a gangster once, reputed, of course." He named him and I let out a low whistle of surprise.

"You said it," Tony said, "Exactly."

"How did that happen? Surely your firm didn't—"

"No." The very thought appeared to amuse him. "No, that was not our style. Some of our clients may have had the same morals, but we only took them on if they had WASP names and the fortunes had been cleaned up for a few generations.

"No, this was only indirectly connected with the firm. I was dragged to a political dinner by a friend doing another friend a favor. You know the kind of thing."

I nodded.

"And this character was there. Something about Wishon's look, his manner, I don't know, something, reminded me of him."

"I know. Something in the eyes, and a feeling of apartness, as if their natural laws are different and we can all go to hell."

Tony nodded, and I went on, "I'd love to find out what he was really doing here."

"What? Doesn't he strike you as someone who'd come to the middle of nowhere just to please a friend, and sit tight just to please a cop?" Tony asked with a grin.

"I don't think he did." I was so relaxed by then, so comfortable, I was ready to tell about my trip to Canada.

When I finished the story he looked at me for a long time, with an expression that was hard to read, and finally said, "I never would have guessed that there is nothing at all that would make you stop when you're following a story."

"It's hard to explain. It's just that I want to—no, I *have* to—find out what's going on. That passion to dig it all up and bring it out into the light of day... well, it just becomes so important sometimes that nothing else seems to matter. Or exist, even." I paused, then added uncomfortably. "Maybe—just maybe—that's connected to my marriage not working out."

Tony smiled. "Or maybe you're just a workaholic. That's a pretty common brand of neurosis. I've certainly seen plenty of it in my profession. As for yesterday, I don't know if I should be more impressed by your guts or your stupidity."

"I know, I know. LaForge read me the riot act."

"I wish you'd be more careful." He put his hand on mine, holding the stem of the wine glass. "Those answers aren't worth this"—he touched my bruise with one finger—"let alone your life."

Maybe he could see from my face that I was about to tell him to mind his own business. He lifted his hand from mine and changed the subject.

"I still wonder if he had anything to do with Terry's death."

"Tony, do you think he killed her?"

Tony shrugged. "Maybe, if he lied about being deeply involved with her. How the hell could she have gotten involved with someone like that anyway? It really makes me wonder what was going on in that mean little mind. She wasn't dumb."

"Maybe she was lonely."

"Women like that are never alone," Tony said flatly.

"I didn't say alone, I said lonely," I answered sharply. I didn't like his tone.

"Hey," he said, lifting his eyebrows, "sounds like you're starting to think of her as a human being. Can't have that. Have a little more to drink."

"What a truly horrid thing to say."

"Yes, wasn't it?" he answered with obnoxious cheerfulness, beckoning to the waiter for another bottle of wine. Then he seemed to notice my expression.

"I'm sorry," he said abruptly. "It *was* horrid. I was being...never mind...I'm too old to play the adolescent smart-ass. I'll stop. Probably it's time to go, anyway."

We talked of other things in the car, and almost recaptured our friendly feelings. At the hotel, he asked, "Are you coming to the funeral? It's tomorrow at eleven."

"So soon?"

"They finished the autopsy, and after that her mother couldn't face calling hours at a funeral home."

"I didn't know they finished the autopsy. Do you know what they found?"

"Pretty much what everyone knew. She was definitely strangled, alcohol in the blood, recent sex."

"I'll be there."

"Notebook in hand?"

"That would be tacky," I said with what I hoped was dignity. "The notes will all be mental."

"Could you stand coming back to my uncle's house afterward? It would give you some material, and frankly," he concluded ruefully. "I could use the moral support."

"Absolutely. Do you think your family will talk to a reporter?"

"I'm sure they won't. Plan to get as much as you can before they figure out who you are," he advised cynically. "Anyway, Maggie will be there. She'll fill you in."

He said good-bye with a friendly hug. "Tomorrow at eleven? St. Matthew's. You remember where it is?"

"The granite church on Elm that looks like a castle?"

"That's it. See you then."

THIRTEEN

Wednesday morning

THE SHOCK OF Terry's death ensured a large turnout
from our class at the funeral. My classmates stood in
front of the church, soberly dressed people in their late
thirties huddled in tight groups as if for comfort. As I
drifted, standing with this group and simultaneously
listening to that one, I learned that there were all sorts
of comfort being sought. People were stunned by the
event, sympathetic to her parents, and, naturally,
deeply upset by the possibility of a murderer among
them. Each person was trying to rationalize the fear in
his or her own way. Some swore it must have been an
unknown intruder, perhaps one of these "New York
soldiers, if you know what I mean." Others took a
quick look around and whispered, "What about that
date of hers?" Some said, reassuring themselves at
least as much as their listeners, "Well, we know we can
count on Al LaForge to deal with it. He's a real solid
lawman. Has anyone heard any news?" A few said,
"Oh, her poor parents..." and the frankly curious
asked each other, "How are they taking it? Does anyone know?" But I noticed that no one said, "Poor
Terry. I'll miss her," "What a friend she was!" "I re-

member the wonderful time we...." No one shed any tears at all.

In the church, of course, it was different. Many older people, presumably family friends, looked stricken. Three grim-faced men with a marked family resemblance sat in front. A woman in elegant black sat between two of them, crying hysterically. I assumed she was Terry's mother. Two other women sat with them, crying quietly. Chris and Sue, Tony, and a number of other people sat immediately behind them, and Maggie hurried in to join them just before the service began.

I spotted the McDowells in the crowd, Richie looking devastated and Laurie appropriately serious, but with something else in her face that did not look like grief to me.

Far in the back of the church, Chief LaForge stood with two men I recognized from my visit to the police headquarters. They all wore appropriate dark suits but their alert stance and watchful eyes, looking everywhere at once, told me they were officers on duty.

The service was mercifully brief. The sermon included comfort to the grieving family, assurances that a just God would right the outrage of Terry's death if earthly authorities could not do so, faith that earthly authorities could do so, and considerable praise for Terry's fine qualities. I could see that the woman up in front had stopped sobbing and was listening intently, nodding her head. Around me, however, in spite of the solemnity of the occasion some of my classmates could not suppress disbelieving grins. I wondered if Tony and Maggie were behaving themselves.

The crowd at the cemetery was smaller. To my surprise, Andy Monroe was there, standing several yards behind the last row in the crowd. He beckoned me over.

I hadn't seen him since our very strange conversation in the parking lot, the night of the reunion. I'd forgotten about him. So much had happened in the few hours and days afterward.

"Why, Andy, I didn't expect to see you here today."

"I didn't know Terry. I mean, not really," he stammered, "but I thought you'd be here. I can never find you at your hotel. You seem to be in and out, in and out, all the time."

"I'm working, Andy," I said as gently as I could, hoping to cover my annoyance. "I'm here to write a story, you know."

"I know," he said resentfully. "Just like before. Then you were always studying. Now you're always working. But—" he cheered up— "maybe you need a ride back? I brought my pickup."

"Oh, Andy, that's sweet of you—"

"I'd do anything just to spend a little time with you. You know," he smiled shyly, "I've even got a picture of you on my dashboard. I cut it out of the yearbook, and I tell the guys it's my girl. It's right up there next to Elvis and my Saint Christopher statue."

"Andy, I'm sorry. I'm going back to Terry's parents' house. And it really is work."

I added, "If your snowplow crew chief called you in an emergency, you'd have to go, wouldn't you? It's kind of like that."

"I see." He nodded. "I would have to go. You're right. I understand now, but Kay, we're going to have at least one date before you go. Whatever it takes. I just know it."

"Yes, Andy, sometime we will."

The crowd at graveside was breaking up by then. Andy said, "Gotta go," and disappeared.

Tony managed to fade back from the crowd to where I stood, and said, "I rode out here with relatives. Can I get a lift back with you?"

In my car he kept crossing and uncrossing his legs and fiddling with the window buttons, the air conditioner, and the radio.

Finally, just to break the tense silence, I said, "How bizarre this is. We were just joking about Cemetery Road Saturday night and now we're here for Terry's funeral."

"She deserved it, Kay," he said wearily. "Oh, not murder. Not really. But she was a clever, mean, heartless little bitch who caused a lot of pain. She got it all back at once."

"Then what has you so wired?"

"The strain of behaving myself while everyone cries and talks about how lovable she was. Acting grief-stricken. Plus last night and this morning with my none-too-lovable family."

He looked and sounded so bleak that I didn't say another word until I had to ask him for directions to Terry's parents' home.

It was a large, handsome stone and shingle house with a spacious lawn, glassed-in sun porch, circular driveway in front, and casement windows.

"Not, I think, the ancestral home?"

"Nope, Chris's folks got that one. This is just an upper bourgeois home of the twenties. My uncle bought it as a wedding gift for his bride." He took a deep breath. "Let's go."

The enormous paneled living room and dining room were already full of people, a subdued babble of voices, smoke, and the clinking of glasses and silverware. The crowd overflowed through French doors onto a stone terrace. Two uniformed maids circulated, picking up ashtrays and used glasses, putting out food and fresh plates.

"Tony, if I'm here I have to say something to her parents," I whispered.

"Oh, sure. Let's go and meet the whole damn family. Why not?"

He led me over to one of the couples from the front of the church. The man was big and beefy, wearing a handsome black suit with gold cuff links and a black-and-blue striped silk tie. He had perfectly cut silver hair, perfectly manicured nails, and hard eyes. The woman was slim, with ash-blond hair in a smooth twist, dressed in a smart black suit with pearls.

"Mother, father, I'd like you to meet Kay Engels, a classmate in town for the reunion."

"I don't remember you from Tony's high-school days. And you stayed for the funeral?" the woman said coolly, with a slight British accent. "How very thoughtful of you."

The man shook my hand, and said, "Behave yourself, Tony, and stay away from the bottles. This is already a distressing enough occasion for us all." He stared at Tony's tie, a somber maroon-and-navy paisley. "Why did you wear that fag tie? Very unsuitable."

"Tony," his mother said, "do be sure to bring your friend back to talk to us later. For now, we have other responsibilities, and you should take her to pay respects to Aunt Dot and Uncle Clarkson."

Tony walked away without another word toward the bar, leaving me to follow. After his glass was refilled he led me to a woman I assumed was Terry's mother and another of the three brothers from the church. This one was equally well-groomed, but his red face and eyes betrayed heavy drinking.

When Terry's mother looked up I was astonished at the resemblance. This was a picture of Terry twenty years down the road. They had the same determinedly blond hair, pink complexion, blue eyes. Even in grief, her careful makeup and White Shoulders perfume insistently proclaimed a girlish femininity. Her expensive-looking dress, clinging black voile, did not conceal a still-attractive, though I suspected seriously corseted, figure.

I took her hand and said, "I'm so sorry for your loss."

"Oh, you dear child, to come and say you're sorry. I don't remember you as a school friend of Terry's, do I? But then, my memory is so bad, and she had so many friends." She started to weep again, and her husband glared at Tony, shooed us away, and put his arms around her, saying indistinctly, "Now, Dottie. Now, Dottie."

As we moved back toward the bar, I realized that there weren't many classmates there. Most of the large crowd appeared to be Terry's parents' friends. They even looked like Terry's parents, prosperous and elderly.

Tony didn't say a word until he had tossed down a drink and started another.

"Good Scotch. Cutty. Nothing but the best in our houses. Want one?"

"No thanks."

"I suppose you feel a pressing need to meet Chris's parents, too," he said.

"No, but I will want to say hello to Chris and Sue."

"Suit yourself," he replied, turning back to the bar for a refill.

"Now, Tony," said a voice behind us, "quit that boozing and come support me while I perform my family duties."

It was Maggie, in a neat black dress and jacket. She hugged us both and said, "Come along, Tony. I need you. Whatever I thought of Terry, that's a pair of parents in pain over there and I've got to go say the right thing."

"Nope," Tony said, signaling for another drink. "I've already done the right thing once—Kay insisted—and I don't have to do it again. It's enough that I'm here."

Maggie gave him a sad, affectionate look and said, "Dear boy, someday you'll grow up. I only hope I'm here to see it."

"Are you trying to say I'm acting immaturely?"

"Figure it out for yourself," she answered and turned away. Taking a deep breath and squaring her shoulders, she went to talk to the bereaved parents, her brother and sister-in-law of forty-plus years.

From across the room, I watched the mime show, as Terry's father shook his sister's hand and Terry's mother smiled wanly, lifted a limp hand in greeting, and then let it drop to her lap. Maggie kissed them both on the cheek and sat with them for a few minutes, but they seemed to have little to say to one another.

I felt a hand at my elbow and looked up into Chris's blue eyes.

"How are you?" he said.

"Fine. How are you and Sue doing?"

"Holding up. Holding up. This whole experience still seems completely unreal. That much is for sure. I'm just glad the kids are at camp."

He steered me toward the bar again. "Come with me while I get a refill. Actually things are a little easier for us now. The shock is still there, but my parents have stepped in to handle the practical details and so on. How about you? Are you heading home soon?"

"Oh, no, I'm staying at least long enough to see how the investigation develops. I'm writing a story about it." He looked startled, but I went on. "I'm thinking of starting another project, too, strictly on spec, not an assignment. It would be a series of articles about changing small-town life, and our generation in particular. I just found there might be more to say than I could in my reunion piece. I must say," I added, "that was a surprise to me."

"How interesting," Chris said at last, looking at me intently. "We were hoping to see more of you, Sue and I. In fact, I have an idea. Just a sec, Susie, come here a minute. Kay is sticking around town for awhile, covering...this business," he said, as he gestured to include the entire room, "but also maybe writing more about our class and so on. What would you think about inviting a few people over one evening and giving her a chance to visit with them in a quiet place? I told the office I won't be in this week, so I'll be around to help."

I protested that Chris was putting Sue in an awful spot, but Sue responded instantly. "It's a great idea. It would be a wonderful break from all this, though," she smiled, "we'd have to be very discreet about it. It wouldn't do to let it get back to the in-laws."

"But Sue, I'm sure it's the worst possible time, and a lot of work—"

"Nonsense. I'd love to do it. Not a bash—that really would be inappropriate—but just a quiet evening, very informal, with old friends." She patted Chris's arm. "Chris knew I'd want to or he wouldn't have asked me in front of you. I think a few of them are still in town visiting, besides the ones who live here, so we should do it quickly, before they leave. Are you free any evening? Then I'll call you as soon as I can put it together. Is that okay?"

"It sounds wonderful."

"I'll talk to you later. Come on, Chris. Duty calls."

Soon the crowd was thinning and Terry's mother was led upstairs for a rest. Going off in search of a bathroom, I blundered into a sort of pantry and straight into an argument between Chris and Tony. They never even noticed that I had knocked lightly and then opened the door a crack, and I was too surprised at first to make a noise.

"For God's sake, Tony! Today of all days—" Chris was saying in a furious whisper.

"Come off it, Chris," Tony replied coldly. "Don't bother putting on a show for me. I know you felt the same way about the dear departed that I did." He poured himself another glass from the bottle he held in his hand.

"I may not have liked her much, but I'm not flaunting it."

"Flaunting it? Is that what I'm doing? Here I thought I was quietly getting drunk in my own little corner, bothering no one. Of course I can't hope to reach your high level of behavior—the perfect master of ceremonies on any occasion, however tragic."

Chris flushed, but said calmly enough, "I'm only trying to help out as much as I can, in a difficult enough situation. Why don't you try it for a change instead of sneering at the whole family?"

By now, Tony was as white as Chris was red. He spoke with exaggerated precision. "Because, cousin Chris, to answer your question, I'm not a hypocrite. And I don't need to prove how perfect I am."

"There's no danger of that."

"Nope. I know it. But I must still be a world-class annoyance to you. Because I know *you're* not perfect either. Because I know a few things about you that would really surprise all those respectful, respectable folks out there, don't I? How far back should I go, Chris?" He suddenly sounded much colder, and a lot less drunk. "Sixth grade? High school? Christmas—junior year in college? You and me? You and Terry?"

I finally dragged myself out of my appalled, fascinated trance and knocked sharply, as if I'd just approached the closed door.

"Tony," I began, "I think it's time I left. Almost everyone seems to be going now."

He walked out of the little room, ignoring Chris, and gripped my arm tightly, saying, "No. Stay awhile.

Please," in a tone that was more commanding than pleading. I'm not sure why I said yes.

Sue, coming down the hall just then, overheard and added with a warm smile, "Please do, Kay. It will be just family soon and—" she looked around swiftly and whispered "it would be such a relief to have someone else here too."

Before long, there was a fresh pot of coffee and sandwiches and cake served to the handful of family members left.

Tony's mother, she of the appraising looks, turned to me and said with a false, bright smile, "You were in Tony's class, yet I don't seem to quite remember you."

"I looked different then," I answered politely.

"Mmm-hmm, I suppose so. But if you're a local girl, perhaps I know your parents. I sometimes think I know everyone. Are they still in town?"

"Oh, no. They moved to Florida right after I graduated. They both passed away many years ago."

"Oh, my. And yet I'm sure I knew someone named Engels here. Or is that your married name?"

With the blandest smile I could manage, and the politest voice, I said, "Engels is my maiden name. My mother sold ladies' lingerie at Jones & Hardy for many years, and my father worked as a foreman at the tool factory. Probably it was a different Engels family."

"Oh, perhaps, perhaps," Mrs. Campbell said airily. "I never said I knew absolutely everyone. So I suppose your parents just scrimped and saved and sent you to a state college or some such place?"

Looking her straight in the eye, I said, "I went to Radcliffe. On a full scholarship."

"How very wonderful for you, my dear. So hard-working and clever. I do admire people who pull themselves up from nothing like that. Of course you do miss the fun side of being young if you have to work that way, don't you? So hard not to turn into a grind. Of course if you have to make your own way in the world.... Fortunately our children—Tony and his cousins—didn't have to. Tony somehow took the notion to become quite the serious student anyway, but I know poor Terry positively partied her way through school."

Controlling my anger, I merely said, "Perhaps I learned more," but I had the satisfaction of a wink from Maggie, and even Sue made a surreptitious clapping gesture.

"Are you that reporter girl?" one of the brothers asked. Between weariness and a couple of drinks, I was having trouble telling them apart. "I've never known a newspaper to report one thing right."

"We do our best—"

He went on as if I'd never spoken. "I think they really are all run by pinkos. Certainly seems that way most of the time."

"Dear," Chris's mother was saying, "let's not get started on politics right now. Please?"

"She's right," one of the other men said, "Forget politics. Whole country's been going downhill since Goldwater lost anyway. Damn Democrats are even making some inroads up here. I want to talk about property, as long as Maggie's honored us with her presence. What the heck's happening with that farm of yours? I understand the state tax fellows shot down that crazy scheme to give it all away."

"You understand wrong, Taylor, as usual. I've been to see them and we worked it all out. I'm going to Arthur's office day after tomorrow and get it all written out, signed, and settled."

"It's a mistake, Maggie. An old piece of property ought to remain in the family, where it's always been. You can't go around giving things away. If people were meant to have property, by God, they ought to have the gumption to get it on their own. Just once, listen to your brothers."

"Fiddlesticks!"

"Maggie, you just don't have a good business head. No woman does. You all get muddleheaded. Now, Clarice has money of her own, and so do Dottie and Louise, and we've taken damn good care of it for them, just as we should have. And no complaints from them, either. They have their nice dividend checks to spend on clothes and decorating and whatnot, and they don't meddle with the business end."

"I'm seventy-three, Taylor," Maggie said, "and you're only sixty-six. I think I'm old enough to know what I'm doing, even if you and Clark and Will don't agree. I have no regrets at all about how I've handled my life *or* my affairs."

"Now, what about you?" she asked, decisively changing the subject. "Are you holding onto your beach house here, or moving down to Palm Beach year-round to be with all the other reactionary old blue-haired golfers?"

Under cover of the ensuing discussion about whether the North Country or Florida was really God's own country, one of the white-haired men beckoned me, very quietly, and walked me across the hall to a study. He wasn't the one with the eyes red from weeping, and he wasn't the one I'd met, so I concluded he must be Chris's father.

Without any polite preliminaries, he said, "Are you writing a story about Terry?"

"Yes, I probably will."

"Well, I don't want you to. Our name's been respected in this county, and even this state, for quite a few generations. We don't want it dragged through the mud now."

"I came to write about going to a reunion, but this is the bigger story." When he didn't say anything, I somehow felt compelled to add, "It's what I do. And after all, Terry was the victim, not the murderer."

He looked right at me. "I know what Terry was. We all do, except her parents, and they don't need to find out by seeing it splashed across the pages of a national scandal sheet. And neither does the rest of this town."

I ignored the slur on *News Now* and what it implied about me and went straight to the main issue.

"Surely the *Falls City Record* will write about it. Why shouldn't I?"

"I can count on them to be . . . tactful. I can't count similarly on you, can I?"

I was sure he couldn't count on the smart local newspaper folks I'd met to sit on the story, and I didn't feel like telling him that he could certainly count on me not to.

When I didn't respond, he said, "How'd you like to have your personal history published in a national rag for the amusement of total strangers?"

"I'm not—"

He went on as if he hadn't heard me. "I know more about you, Miss Engels, than you might expect. You see, I'm the man who arranged your adoption."

I felt as if the room had just tilted, and I would fall out of my chair if I didn't hold on tight.

"What did you say?" The words felt like screaming in my throat, but my ears heard them come out as a whisper.

"Your adoption. I realized it when you described your parents. I'm a lawyer, you know."

I had the impression then that he actually saw me for the first time. Perhaps my shock showed in my face.

"You don't know?" I shook my head, speechless. "They said they didn't want you to know, but you don't mean they kept it a secret all those years?" I nodded. "Damn fools."

He smiled slightly. I wouldn't call it a warm smile.

"Maybe we can come to an agreement. If you'd like to know all about this, and I imagine you would, I could send you a package with all the records when you're back in New York, and after a witnessed, notarized promise that you won't write the story is sitting on my desk. The adoption was all arranged through me. I'm sure there's no one else still alive who knows a thing about it."

"I can't do that," I managed to say. "My boss knows all about it. I have to give him a story now."

"I see." He paused. "All right then, a copy of your published, very, very discreet story. How's that? I imagine you'd like to know a few things right now."

I had to get out of there. I stood up, said as calmly as I could, "I'll think it over," and walked out.

Tony followed me to the car. He had the desperate look of a horse about to bolt, and I'm sure I looked exactly the same.

"I almost suggested dinner, but I may not be able to get free. And I won't be fit company even if I can."

"It's okay," I said distractedly. "I need to be alone right now."

"Same here. I'm planning to go home as soon as I can, and get as drunk as I possibly can," he said with a bitter smile. "My family has that effect on me."

"I can see why; they're really something. But is that the best way to deal with it?"

"Don't be a social worker, Kay! There's no best way, no good way, no way at all except running away. I should know. I've been doing it all my life."

He left me, then turned back and said in a different voice, "I'm sorry. I'm being obnoxious. I'll be all right tomorrow. Thanks for coming."

He put his hand under my chin, kissed me swiftly, and went back into the house.

FOURTEEN

I STARTED THE car and drove. I just drove, faster and faster, and it must have been an hour before I realized I had been driving aimlessly, speeding along outside the city with no direction at all. When I finally stopped on some deserted country road I was dry-eyed but shaking, and I had no idea where I was.

I got out and paced back and forth, trapped in such a whirlpool of feelings that I didn't know what to do with myself first. I even hit the car with my fist a few times. The pain shocked me into starting to focus on what I had just heard.

I was adopted. He said I was adopted. Was he telling the truth? Was that remotely possible? He certainly wanted something from me, and I was sure he was ruthless. But it would be an absurd tactic if it weren't true. And he'd first mentioned the adoption in passing, as if taking it for granted that I knew. He only tried to bribe me with his knowledge later.

How could I *not* know? How could my parents have kept it from me, all those years? How had they managed it? And why? Standing out there in the dark, in that clean, earth-smelling country air under bright stars, leaning against the car without moving, I was breathing hard, almost unable to breathe at all. I was trying to sort through memories twenty and thirty years old. How far back could I reach? I closed my eyes, wrapping my arms around myself in the late-night chill. How deep could I go?

There were baby pictures. Eventually I might remember where they were stored.

My mother always told me I was born on March 14 in Rome, New York, at a private maternity hospital that was no longer there. That much I knew, and that's what my birth certificate said. When had I last seen it, anyway? Last time I renewed my passport? I was sure—*sure*—that there were no surprises there.

What else? I had no memory of my mother talking about her pregnancy, but why would I? I was never one of those little girls who were interested in babies, and maybe—maybe—she had a way of discouraging those questions. Something in her voice and face, something that gently but firmly closed a door. I had thought it was prudishness, once I was old enough to think about it at all. Now I thought maybe it was something else.

Had I ever pretended I was adopted, as many kids do? Had my mother ever even used the word in my presence? Growing up, did I know anyone who was adopted? I couldn't remember. I just couldn't dig that deep.

In the dark, my own words came back to me: "like turkeys who'd hatched a parrot." And I think it was in that moment that I began to believe it was true.

The questions continued to go around and around in my mind, but more and more slowly. My eyes were seeing everything in a blur, and when I looked at my watch, I was shocked to see that it was after one in the morning. It had been a long, hard day. If I didn't find my way back to the hotel soon I'd fall asleep lying across the hood of the car.

Shaking my head hard to wake up, I looked around me for the first time and saw that I was on a hill, with the lights of the city below and to the left. Pointing the car toward the lights, I knew I could find my way home. Strangely enough, home is what I thought.

I slept from sheer exhaustion, but badly, with dreams that haunted every sleeping moment.

My father and mother were there, but their faces faded in and out, shifting and changing. And I was there, too. I watched myself in the dream, looking in a mirror, and my face faded in and out too. Then I seemed to go into the mirror, and met, not Alice, but Mr. Campbell, grinning like a cat and curled up like a caterpillar on a mushroom.

"Shouldn't you turn into a parrot?" I asked.

"Oh, no, I don't turn into that." Then he grinned and grew another head, and another, and another, and they all turned into dragon heads but I still knew each of them was Campbell. I grabbed each one and shook it and shook it, and a new one grew in its place. None of them ever told me anything.

Thursday morning

I WOKE UP AT LAST, and the instant I was fully conscious there was one word in my mind: *who?* If my parents weren't my parents, who were? Beneath that single word, there were a lot of other thoughts rolling around. I couldn't understand how my parents had kept it a secret for so long, and I couldn't begin to imagine why. And I was just barely beginning to realize how angry I was at their lifelong lie.

Not to mention the anger I felt at Mr. Campbell. I wasn't even thinking, then, of accepting his offer, but I was furious at him for offering it.

And my jaw still hurt. But right on top of all those layers of feelings lay that simple, one-word question.

Now, how was I going to answer it? There was no one I could ask, and that was probably part of how the secret had been kept. I had always been amazed at, and a little envious of, my classmates, who were in their cousins' weddings, complained about Christmas dinners at Grandma's with "the whole family," spent summer vacations traveling to see distant relatives. My parents were old when I was born. They had already lost one parent each by then, and my remaining grandparents died when I was still quite small. Of each of them I have only the dimmest of memories. They are hardly even memories, more like emotions I remember feeling.

My grandmother, my mother's mother, scared me. I remember a harsh voice and critical eyes. My paternal grandfather died when I was four, and I do remember just a little more—sitting on his lap and playing with his old-fashioned pocket watch, patting his bald, shiny head, and singing silly songs with him. What few memories remain with me are all warm ones.

My mother was an only child, and my father's one brother was killed in the Battle of the Bulge.

There was no one else. Both my parents came from small families. Cousins were scattered. One had been stationed in California during the war and stayed out there. Another had married a Kansas boy who was stationed at Camp Oake and settled with him in Topeka. Another worked for a local factory that relocated to Georgia in 1947, and he went with it. Like my parents, none of them were travelers or writers, and they'd all lost touch. I didn't even know their names. There was no one I could ask.

My parents' social life had been very casual. People they bowled with, people they played cards with. I couldn't think of one person I could describe as an intimate friend, someone my mother might have confided in. Not one person whose friendship went way back, who might have been around when they adopted me. There was no one I could ask.

I knew adoption records can only be unsealed with a court order, and then only with an enormously powerful reason. I remembered that from a story in the magazine. Campbell had as much as told me he was the only one who'd been involved. There was no one I could ask.

Well, I wasn't ready to accept that. There had to be someone. I just hadn't figured out who. And somewhere, there was a big box of my mother's papers, too.

After my father died, unexpectedly, my mother told me for the first time that she had a heart condition. She might be around for years or might not, and she gave me the name of the lawyer in Florida who had her will and all the instructions about disposing of her property. I was in college, studying hard, and she didn't want me to have to be bothered with all those problems if it happened suddenly. It did happen that way, only six months later, and the lawyer made the arrangements, stored what she wanted kept, and disposed of all the rest. All I had to do was go to the funeral. A few months later, he sent me a small check and an accounting, and that was the last time I thought about those matters for a long time.

Years later, when I was overseas, I got a form letter explaining that the lawyer was retiring and asking whether I wanted my papers sent to me or transferred to a storage facility. Of course I chose storage, and when I returned to the States, some years later, it never even crossed my mind to see what was in the boxes. Nothing interesting, I was sure. And I had forgotten about them. But somewhere in my files at home, I had the records. So somewhere in a warehouse in central Florida, there might be some answers. Great. It could be weeks before I could get home to deal with this. I was considering a quick weekend trip back to New York when the phone rang.

It was Sue Campbell. "I'm taking a chance that you might be free for lunch. My in-laws are helping Terry's folks get settled at the cottage, and I'd love to have a break from family. Maybe we can plan that get-together we talked about yesterday."

I was hungry and it suddenly sounded like a good idea. I didn't stop to think about whether I was in a fit state for socializing. Sue suggested I come over rather than go out, and that certainly suited me.

I looked as drained as I felt, but I did the best I could, and thought I made a presentable appearance in my new black skirt and the tan, black, and cream silk camp shirt from my traveling outfit.

We ate in Sue's sunny pastel kitchen, where flowers on the table matched the flowered cloth napkins. Over Bloody Marys and shrimp salad Sue confessed, "I know I should be mournful, but I have about used up those feelings. The murder is as shocking and dreadful as can be, but I've spent the last four days being appropriately grief-stricken over someone I really didn't even like. Whew, am I glad to escape.

"Now tell me how your story is going, and how we can help. Should we do this party?"

I tried to concentrate on her questions and talk coherently, but I couldn't quite manage it.

"Kay, what's wrong?" Sue finally asked with real concern. "You're so distracted, and you look upset. Please let me help."

She said it with so much warmth that I just broke down and poured out the whole story, never stopping to think that Campbell was her father-in-law.

"Well," she said after a long silence, "I'm certainly shocked, though not half as shocked as you must be." She gripped my hand. "Try to believe they must have done it out of love. But my father-in-law—" She shook her head slowly and seemed to be struggling for words.

"You have to understand...well, it's not right, what he said to you...I know it's not...but family, that whole idea of the Family Name, means a lot to them, his generation... There's not a lot of real family warmth there, and Chris and I are raising our boys quite differently...but family does mean a lot, they just express it differently—" She stopped when she saw my unforgiving expression.

"Oh, dear, this doesn't mean a thing to you, does it? Maybe you have to be part of the family to see it. And I do know he was wrong to try to bully you—he's a man who's used to having his own way." She frowned and shook her head. "Don't I know it! But this is really—well, it's cruel. There's no other name for it." She thought another moment. "I sort of have an idea. Let me think it over while I get coffee and dessert." She started to clear the table, and then came back with a manila envelope.

"I almost forgot. I have some of the reunion pictures back, and I thought they might be useful for you to see. Or amusing anyway."

I looked through them idly, not really focusing. At the moment stories, murders, and reunions all seemed equally unimportant.

After a while, though, the pictures did begin to catch my interest. The awards ceremony; the old cheerleading squad, clowning and showing some leg; middle-aged basketball players in suits, leaping for a jump ball; the longtime couples dancing in the spotlight—

I looked again at that one. There was Laurie McDowell, in a pale green net concoction, very junior-prom, with a hair ornament perched over her blond bun. It was a stiff bow with flowers attached, and I had last seen it in the hands of a hotel chambermaid. That was what I had been trying to remember ever since the exercise class, that ornament in Laurie's hair.

"Sue, can I borrow this for a day or two?" I needed to have a talk with Chief LaForge.

"Oh, sure, I have the negatives."

She came into the dining ell and said, "I've thought it over. I'll talk to Dad—my father-in-law, that is—and see if I can persuade him to be more reasonable. Sometimes I can cajole him when no one else can. Let me try."

"Oh, Sue, I'd be so grateful!"

She smiled. "I can't promise anything, but I'll do what I can. Why, your mother could still be alive, and dying to see you. How could I *not* help? Now, eat your dessert, skip the coffee, and go back to bed. That's the mother in *me* speaking. You look just about done in."

She was right. I went back to the hotel, thankful for her understanding, and threw myself on the bed gratefully for a long nap.

FIFTEEN

I DIDN'T REALLY get to sleep. Tony called just as I was drifting off.

"Kay, I've been phoning for a couple of hours. Didn't you get your messages?"

"No, I didn't even check," I said, looking at the flashing light on the phone. "I spent the morning—"

"No, wait," he interrupted, in a choking voice. "I have something to tell you. I'm out at Maggie's. Kay." His voice started to break. "Kay, she died last night."

"*What* did you say?"

"She died. Last night. A neighbor found her. He comes in the morning to help with chores. They think it looks like an accidental insulin overdose—he found her in the kitchen, dressed—insulin things out. He called me and I...we...called the ambulance service and went in to town with her...sheriff had to come out to take a look so I came back...I'm still here now. I don't know what else to do."

"Oh, Tony." My eyes filled with tears. "How awful. I hardly knew her and it even hurts me. Are you...I mean, is there anything I can do?"

"I would love company. Would you consider coming out?"

"I'm on my way."

When I arrived at Maggie's, Tony folded me into a long hug. I could feel him shaking as he held me. His face looked as if he hadn't slept in days.

"Been a hell of a week, hasn't it?" He looked with distaste at the Camel he had just lit and said, "I haven't smoked in years, but the place just doesn't seem like Maggie's without the smell of her cigarettes." After a few puffs he threw it away and said, "Kay, something is wrong here. You saw her. Did she seem like a fuddled old lady to you?"

"No, you know she didn't. But late at night and tired, with the strain of the funeral? Who knows?"

"I don't believe it," he said flatly. "I can't believe it. She suggested I drive out with her after the funeral, maybe spend the night. 'Funerals are so melancholy,' she said. I knew she was thinking of Harry, but I also thought she was trying to take care of me, and I said no. I was in such a foul mood by then, I didn't think even she could stand me. At least, that's what I said. The truth is, I just wanted to go indulge myself in self-pity and resentment. If I'd been here—" He didn't have to finish. The bleakness and guilt in his eyes said it all.

"But Tony—"

"Kay. Listen. There was a bottle of brandy on the table, a glass with lipstick on it, alcohol smell on her breath. The sheriff figures she had a drink or two, enough to confuse her, gave herself the wrong insulin dose, and went into shock."

"There's a reaction diabetics get that changes their breath—" I said.

He shook his head. "Insulin shock. Different smell. This was brandy, they said." He met my eyes. "You know, and I know, she didn't drink. She said so the night you were here. I know for a fact she hasn't had a drop in ten years. Why last night, after the funeral of a niece she didn't even like?"

"Goddamn," I said softly. "Good question."

Tony nodded. "Something doesn't feel right. Help me look around?"

"Yes. What are we looking for?"

"I don't know. Something, anything, that feels funny."

The living room looked just the same as when we last had seen it. A coffee cup on one table. Magazines were stacked on the floor and several books lay open, face-down, on the sofa. Under the sofa lay a pair of black heels, looking as though Maggie had just come in and kicked them off. Tony carefully put the books back on the shelves and picked up the shoes.

In the kitchen the table was clear. Tony said, "The sheriff took the bottle and glass and the syringe."

There were a few breakfast dishes in the sink. Curdled milk in the bowl told us they'd probably been there since yesterday. Tony washed them carefully and put them away. He reddened under my questioning look. "It's the last thing I can do for her," he said.

In the bedroom the bed was made and a nightgown and robe hung neatly on a hook, but makeup was scattered on the dresser and black stockings with a run lay in the wastebasket under the cellophane wrapping from a fresh pair.

House tidied, lights out, water turned off, we went out on the porch and sat in the late-afternoon sun, holding hands, staring into Maggie's wood and saying very little. Quite suddenly I saw a face in the woods staring back at me.

It was a man with black eyes and a deeply tanned, deeply lined face. He stood for a long moment, absolutely still and absolutely silent. When he stepped forward at last I saw that he was of medium height and powerful build, erect bearing, dressed in shabby work clothes.

"You are a friend of Maggie's?" he asked with an air of quiet self-confidence.

Tony turned and the man said, "You are Tony, Maggie's nephew."

"Yes. And you? Are you Chief Smith?"

He nodded. "I hoped you would come. I must tell you about Maggie."

Instantly alert, Tony said, "Would you like to come in? Sit and talk?"

"No, thank you. I'll tell you what I have to say and then go. They say Maggie's death was an accident. I have heard this. I say it was not."

"What?" Tony turned his head sharply to look into the old man's face. "What did you say?"

"I visited her last night. We talked. She was not confused in her mind, and she was not drinking. It was no accident. I am sure."

"Are you?" Tony said. "Are you sure it isn't just that you can't believe it really happened? None of us can."

The chief looked unimpressed with this reasoning. "She was my friend. I know what I know, but there is more. She had a visitor here, after I left. I was camping here on the farm for a few days. I heard the car and saw the lights. The car was a dark color. I could not see who was in it, but I heard voices, hers and another. A man."

"Have you told anyone else?"

There was a faint glint of something like humor in the man's eyes. "Who would I tell? The police, when they were here? Who would take me seriously, me, an old Indian who did not even see what kind of car it was or who was in it? Only you, perhaps, who loved Maggie and had her trust. Find out for her."

He turned to go, but Tony said, "Wait. Where can I find you if I need to know more?"

"Tonight I will camp here near her home, mourning in my own way, all alone. She was a true friend. I will never know anyone else like her. Perhaps I will be at the funeral with a few others, but you will not see us. After that, look for me on the reservation." And then he was gone.

"I knew it, Kay! I knew it. It was so demeaning to her, the picture the sheriff drew of some muddleheaded old thing tight on a little too much brandy. There is something else, all right."

"I hate to throw cold water," I said slowly, "but what he said doesn't really prove a thing."

"I know. I know, but it proves something to me. And it gives me something to go on. Not much," he admitted. "A man with a dark car could be anyone at all. My father, for instance, with his black Lincoln, or Chief LaForge, or her neighbor down the road. He's got a brown Ford, I think."

"Does anyone gain anything at all from her death?"

"Only Chief Smith and his tribe, as far as I know. Maggie can't have had a whole lot of money socked away, and she was leaving most of it to them, to maintain the farm. The land's not worth much on the market. There are more farms than farmers available around here. I think she planned to leave some jewelry and stuff to people in the family."

"Just the same, it might be worthwhile to have a look at her will."

Tony nodded wearily. "I'll do it first thing in the morning. I know her lawyer. And I'll start making a list of every male acquaintance of Maggie's with a dark car."

"You don't mean to try to trace the whereabouts of all of them, do you? There could be dozens."

"Got a better idea?"

I shook my head. "It just seems farfetched to me. It's such a thin thread." I thought, but didn't say, that it sounded to me as if Tony's guilt was doing the reasoning rather than his good sense.

"In the meantime," he said, "I'm ready to go. I keep having this feeling that Maggie will come around the corner of the house any minute." His voice shook a little.

"I know. Where to? Have you eaten?"

"Eaten? No," he said with some surprise. "I don't think I ate at all today. I was too blitzed this morning and then too upset to even think about food." He grinned suddenly and shook his head. "And wouldn't Maggie have scoffed at that. She's probably somewhere up there right now saying, 'Don't be a fool, Tony. Starving yourself won't bring me back. Go eat a hamburger and stay off the booze. You can't handle it when you're depressed.'"

I had to smile. "Is that what she'd say to you?"

"Sure. She did say things just like that, many times. She'd be right, too. She always was. How about coming to my place and I'll throw a couple of hamburgers on the grill?"

While Tony cooked he told me stories about Maggie, wonderful, funny stories, and I felt new admiration for the woman and real sorrow that I would never know her any other way.

Tony served up the food with a flourish. He'd managed to throw a passable salad together from canned vegetables, odds and ends in the refrigerator, and good olive oil, and with French bread from the freezer it made a decent spur-of-the-moment meal. We ate at the picnic table on the tiny lawn, watching the sunset behind the islands and letting the dark surround us until we could barely see each other.

Later I stood on the dock and looked up at the sky, brilliant with stars and a low-riding, perfectly round moon, and said, "It never fails to amaze me. We don't see them at all in the city. And the silence. It's so deep, it almost makes a noise itself."

Tony put his arms around me and kissed me. It was a good kiss, warm and sweet, suggesting more than demanding. When he stopped, he moved his head back just enough to give me one of his questioning looks. "How did that feel to you?"

I said shakily, "It felt like something I'd been waiting for all these years." I took a deep breath and gently pulled away from him, turning to look at the water. I couldn't look into his eyes. "That doesn't make sense. I never had any romantic feelings about you, never. It was always—" I stopped before I said, "Chris," and finished, "it was always friendship. I don't understand it."

"Neither do I," he said from behind me. "Except for one thing. When I think back, the few times I ever said anything real or important in class, I felt as if I was talking straight to one person. And that person was you."

"I'm scared," I said in a tight little voice.

"So am I," he said, surprising me. "No one I know here interests me. You do, and I don't know what that means. What's scaring you?"

"The possibility of being too involved, and ending up miserable. Of it being just a pass for you, after all, but not for me. Or for me and not for you, and feeling like a bitch. Of neither of us giving a damn. I've been to all those places before, and I'm sick to death of emotional complications. I'd rather have no love life at all."

"Kay," he said, not moving from where he stood, "maybe we ought to just let this, whatever it is, grow a little. I don't think the danger is feeling too little. Do you? Really?"

"No," I said softly.

"Then let's go back to town now and give it a little time. I'll be here. You'll be here for a while. We have Terry's killer to thank for that, at least. We can wait. Knots have a way of untangling themselves sometimes." His voice sounded less assured than his words.

I turned and gave him a shaky smile. "I feel like a fool."

"That's okay. I do too. Do you suppose we'll ever get over it?" He gave me a wry smile and I nodded.

We were almost back at the hotel before I worked up the nerve to ask, "Are you angry?"

"No." He reached over and covered my hand with his. "Disappointed, yes. Angry, no. Let me prove it by taking you to dinner tomorrow night."

He walked me from the car to the door of my room, then stood there like a boy, brushing stray strands of my hair from my forehead with one gentle finger.

"Tony..." At a loss for words, I put both hands behind his neck and kissed him good night. Then I went in quickly and closed the door.

Alone in my room, I sat up for quite a while looking out at the garden, trying to decide if I was the world's biggest fool or a mature adult at last applying some intelligence to my emotional life. Giving it up at last, I finally went to bed. It was only when I was at the edge of a troubled sleep that I remembered Chris's warning words about Tony and wondered how much they had affected my behavior.

SIXTEEN

Friday morning

WHEN CHIEF LAFORGE arrived at his office the next morning, I was waiting for him with the photograph of Laurie in my hand. "I have something important to tell you."

Ignoring my words, he said, "How's that bruise on your jaw? Been over to Canada lately?"

"Of course not. Now can you please listen—"

"Come on in the office. I've got a couple of things to say to you."

He shuffled forms on his desk for a moment, and then, without looking up, said, "By the way, we arrested Tony Campbell late last night."

"I don't believe it."

He looked up then, directly at me. "It's true. We got a witness. We found the kid who delivered that last drink to Terry Campbell. He said not only was she alive then, but Tony was with her. He gave us a positive ID. Looks to me like no one else ever had a chance to do it after that. And Campbell lied to us."

"But . . . but . . ." I sat down. My mind was whirling. "Wait a minute. Didn't you say you knew what time the drink order came in? When was that?"

"Twelve-ten, the bartender says."

"At twelve-ten, Tony was dancing with me."

"One: How do I know you aren't just saying that?" He held up a hand to stop my indignant protest. "And two: The kid confessed he didn't deliver the drink right away. He stopped in the john and had a smoke on the way, so the drink took longer to get there than you would expect. Now you can argue if you have to."

"It doesn't make any sense," I said. "*Why* would he? Do you have any kind of reason?"

"Not yet, but if it's there we'll find it."

"It's not really proof anyway," I argued. "The waiter didn't witness the murder."

"True, but it's the best we've got so far, and we're going with it. We'll find the rest, now that we know which way to look. I admit," he went on, "my money really was on Wishon originally. What did you have to tell me that's so important?"

"You need to know about something I found out yesterday, because it suggests another possible suspect. What would you say to proof that someone else, someone with a first-class reason and the strength to kill her, was in the hall right in front of Terry's room that night?"

He looked at me suspiciously. "What are you getting at?"

"I have part of the proof right here in this picture, and I know where the rest is," I said quietly. "Try to listen and keep your feelings out of it."

"You're out of line, miss. Just say what you came to say."

"I'm talking about Laurie McDowell. She lost her hair ornament in front of Terry's room. A maid found it there and showed it to me. Here's a picture showing Laurie wearing it."

The chief flushed angrily, but he only said, "So what?"

"It might make you ask some questions."

"That's all nonsense. She's a small woman, a kid. It takes a lot of muscle to kill someone that way. It has to be a big, strong person."

"Didn't you ever see Laurie lead an exercise class? I went to one the other day. She's stronger than most men of any size. And besides that, couldn't hate take the place of strength when it comes to killing someone? We both know Laurie had more than enough reason for that."

"*If* she knew about Terry and her husband. Only if she knew." I continued to look straight at him. "All right," he admitted. "She probably knew."

"What are you going to do about it?"

"Talk to the maid," he said resignedly. "Look at those pictures. Do you know the maid's name?"

I told him and he jotted the information down. "Maybe I'll talk to Laurie, depending on what I hear. But this doesn't get Campbell out. Not even close."

I nodded. "May I see Tony?"

The chief looked thoughtful, then nodded. "Okay. You won't be left alone with him. Davis!" he called. "Take Miss Engels to see Tony Campbell." He turned away abruptly and sat staring at the names he had just written on his note pad.

Davis led me to a room in another part of the building and brought Tony in. He looked pale, with a twenty-four hour growth of stubble and circles under his eyes. We talked softly and rapidly.

"Kay! How did you find out about this idiocy?"

"I came to see the chief about something else. Why? Doesn't anyone else know?"

"Not yet, I hope. Only my lawyer," he said ruefully. "I called an old friend in New York who used to be in the DA's office. He'll be here this afternoon. I'll be sprung by tonight."

"How the hell did this happen?"

"I don't know. I've been up most of the night trying to figure it out. Roger's going to have some tough questions for everyone involved as soon as he gets here. And in the meantime I'm stuck in here and I can't find out anything about Maggie. Kay, *please*, can you ask some questions for me?"

"Yes, of course. No, wait a minute. What am I saying?" I was appalled at my own quick response. I was supposed to be covering this story, not becoming a figure in it. I was supposed to ask my own questions, not someone else's. I had to think.

Tony waited anxiously without saying anything until I said, finally, "At this point, there isn't much difference between what you want to know and what I do. I'm not even sure just what the story really is anymore, so I have to ask everyone questions, I guess. For now, anyway, I'll help. Do you want me to talk to Maggie's lawyer? Who and where? What else?''

"Could you find the kid from the hotel who says I was in Terry's room? Something's really wrong there. No, wait. He's lying, and you might scare him. Let my lawyer do it, officially. If you could just find him.

"Oh, God, Kay, so much has happened, I can't even think straight anymore. Back in the days when I was a wild kid,'' he said grimly, "my parents used to say I would end up in jail. So here I am. I suppose they'll be here later. How gratifying for them that they turned out to be right." He stopped abruptly, then said, "That's not really the main thing on my mind. I'm just babbling. I've been talking to myself since the middle of the night. I didn't sleep much in here. What brought you down here anyway?''

I told him, and was rewarded by the look in his eyes. "It could be," he said. "It certainly could be. God knows she had more reason to do it than I did."

"Tony, I've got to get to work. I'll stop by later.'' I couldn't wait to go. I knew I should have been asking Tony probing journalistic questions, or at the very least intelligent ones, but all I wanted to do was hold his hand. I resented this. Just to complete my confusion, the thought kept flickering in and out that perhaps he really was guilty and I was being conned. I'm not conned easily, and the very possibility made me even more resentful.

I met Chris Campbell on the steps of the jail.

"Kay!"

"Hello, Chris. How've you been?"

"Pretty awful. This week has been one crisis after another. And now Tony."

"How did you know?"

"Small town. Word gets around. I haven't called his parents yet. I'm just going in now to see if there's anything he needs."

"Chris, doesn't it seem impossible to you? Tony as a killer?"

"The impossible part was that someone was killed. Tony? I just don't know. He's a funny guy, Kay. Always has been. Very, let's say, unpredictable. Maybe I mean unstable. Someone who might explode someday, perhaps. But yes, it's hard to believe there might be a killer in the family. Then again, it's hard to believe there's a killer's victim in the family."

"Maybe two," I said, longing to confide in someone I could trust. "Tony doesn't believe Maggie's death was an accident. We met Chief Smith at Maggie's house. He says she had a visitor that night, quite late. He heard a man's voice, and saw a dark car in the driveway. He really believes, and Tony does too, that Maggie was murdered."

"Tony says that?" Chris asked with some surprise. "He thinks someone is out to decimate the Campbells? That's strange. He'd be the only one with anything to gain from Maggie's death. I'm sure she left everything to him. He was always her favorite."

"But—"

"She never finished that loony plan to give it all back to the Indians." He looked at me, and the whole collection of emotions I was struggling with must have showed on my face. "Are you involved with helping Tony?"

I could feel myself turning red, and answered with extra vehemence, "Certainly not. I'm trying to write a story."

"I see." He went on gently, "He isn't worth it, you know. Trust me. I've known him all our lives." He continued briskly. "Sue and I have neglected you. We never did manage to arrange that little party we talked about. I apologize, but I'm sure you understand. You were alone here and Tony, I bet, has moved right in to fill the empty hours. Have dinner with us tonight," he urged. "We'll forget about all this mess, including Tony, talk about old times, steal a few hours of fun. What do you say?"

I tried to say that they were under no obligation, that they had far too much to do and think about, and no time to be bothered with entertaining, but Chris finally said, "Please. *We'd* appreciate it. We'll go out. Pick you up about six-thirty."

I finally said yes.

I spent the next few irritating and futile hours trying to find the waiter whose information had put Tony in jail. I reminded myself, more and more grimly as the day wore on, that I wasn't doing it for Tony. It was a legitimate part of the story.

Either the hotel staff had been strictly warned by the police or this waiter was an exceptionally close-mouthed individual. At the end of two hours I knew his name, Earl Mayhew, and that was all. No one knew where he lived. No one could remember how long he'd worked there, or if he had a family, or where he hung out. One waitress said something vague about a trailer park on Miller Creek Road, but she didn't know, or wouldn't say, more than that. The manager admitted to knowing the answers to most of my questions, but he refused point-blank to share them with me. And neither charm nor guile nor suggested monetary displays of gratitude produced answers from anyone else.

I gave up, at least for a while, and called Arthur Langton, Maggie's lawyer.

SEVENTEEN

Friday afternoon

ARTHUR LANGTON TURNED out to be an old man, perhaps older than Maggie, with shaky hands and sharp eyes. "I don't mind talking to you. Tony called and said to do it, but he didn't say why. I've known Maggie most of my life, you know, and all of hers. Our parents were close friends. First time I saw her, I was six years old and she was a newborn baby in a cradle. Did Tony tell you I proposed to her three times? No? Maybe he doesn't know. Maggie wasn't the kind to kiss and tell, though there never was a whole lot of kissing involved.

"First time was just before she went out West. She was just back from Vassar, the prettiest thing, and the most determined. I did everything I could to persuade her, but no, she had her heart set on a change of scene. So I married a gal who was more of a hometown girl, and we were happy enough. She died in her forties, though. Had a bad heart. A year or so later, Maggie turned up in town for a visit.

"Well, she was middle-aged by then, just like me, and she was still the prettiest thing, deep tan and slim as a girl. So I tried again. Nope. I was her dear friend, but her life was out there.

"Ha! Six months later, she came home with that professor of hers." He stopped and looked at a spot above my head and long ago.

"I shouldn't have put it like that. He was a good man and I liked him in spite of his being married to Maggie. After he died, I thought, 'Two lonely old people, why not?' She wouldn't hear of it. Said she was flattered but it wouldn't be fair to me. Said she couldn't care about me the way I deserved."

His eyes, fixed on that empty spot on the wall, glistened when he added, "If she'd said yes, maybe I could have taken care of her. Maybe she'd be home right now, cooking my dinner, instead of laid out at a funeral home."

He looked sharply at me and said in a different voice, "Just what is it you want to know? And why didn't Tony come himself?"

I answered the second question first. Langton exploded. "That young fool!"

"I don't think this is Tony's fault."

"Not Tony! Well, yes, Tony's a young fool too. If he didn't have a history with LaForge from his wild oat days, I don't for a minute believe he'd be in jail now. But no, I meant Al LaForge. I know Tony too well to swallow this story. LaForge has messed up somehow."

"How do you think?" I asked, cheered up by his vehemence.

"How the heck should I know? Asked the wrong questions, or asked the wrong people, or walked right past evidence any fool could see. I've known Al since he was a young cop wet behind the ears. Means well. Works hard. But he doesn't have enough curiosity. Understand what I mean? He settles for the first answers, not necessarily the best. I hope Tony's got a good lawyer. I gave up criminal practice as a sixty-fifth birthday present to myself. He's not stupid enough to try to handle it himself, is he?"

"Oh, no, he has a criminal law friend on the way up from New York."

"Glad to hear it," he said. "Now, down to business. You'd better tell me the truth. I'll pay Tony a little visit this evening and check it all with him anyway."

As I told him the story, he nodded slowly. "Could be," he said. "Could be. I don't see Maggie making a mistake with her insulin. She was every bit as sharp the day she died as when she was twenty. I don't know who'd want to hurt her, though. Not that she was an angel. If you got on her wrong side she'd let you know, and you'd feel skinned alive for quite some time, too, but no one gets killed for having a sharp tongue, except by a spouse, maybe. Not when they have a good heart along with it."

"Tony and I wondered if there was anyone who stood to gain by her death. That's why he sent me to you."

"You mean you'd like to hear about her will? I suppose I can tell. I'm the executor anyway. Her plan for giving the farm to Chief Smith's tribe wasn't ever finished. Matter of fact, she was supposed to come in just yesterday." He had to take a deep breath before he could go on. "She was supposed to come in and sign the final draft. Strictly speaking, her old will is still in effect."

"And that was...?"

"I drew it up for her years back, when she suddenly became an aunt three times in one year. She never did change it, not even after they were grown and had their own families, even though I knew she liked some of those kids less than others. Just never got around to it, I guess."

"And it specified?" I controlled my impatience, but only with an effort.

"Why, she left everything to the children, divided three ways." I coughed to cover an enormous smile of relief that I knew was spreading to my face. "Never changed it when she got married. Didn't need to. Harry had some money of his own, and they felt hers belonged in her family."

"What happened if one of the three died before she did?"

He looked sharply at me. "You mean the way it did happen? Divided in half for the other two. She wasn't thinking about their heirs when she wrote it. They were just babies then, and as I said, she never bothered about it afterward.

"But you have to understand, we're not talking about much here. Farms are dirt cheap in the North Country, if you'll pardon the pun. It's harder than ever to make a living farming. Land values haven't gone up in years. And she didn't have a lot of money left. What she had would have come in handy for Chief Smith and his folks, but altogether it's not enough to mean much to people like Tony or Chris."

"Are you sure about that?"

"Sure about Tony. I've seen his tax returns. He's doing very well, alimony and all. I don't know the same for Chris for absolute fact, but if he isn't prospering, he's fooling everyone in town. So the answer is no, there is no one who gains a thing they want or need by Maggie's death. We only lose." He looked at me fiercely, as if daring me to disagree.

"I know," I said softly.

"If you don't have any more questions," he said, staring again at that spot on the wall, "I'd just as soon be alone now. I'll go see Tony in a while."

"I understand. I have to be going anyway. Thanks for your time and information. I appreciate it." I didn't know what else to say to the dignified old man sitting there all alone. He waved me out without getting up or even looking at me again.

Back in my room I felt guilty, thinking of Tony in jail while I was getting ready to go out to dinner. Then I was annoyed with myself, and with him, for feeling guilty. After all, I spent all afternoon trying to get some answers for him. And I didn't owe him a thing anyway. And his lawyer probably had him out by now. I certainly had a right to a pleasant dinner with old friends. And then I thought that I'd call him, at least, and then I wondered why I thought I should.

When Chris came he was alone in the car. "Susie's stuck at the lake," he said, "so I'm a lonely bachelor tonight. You don't mind keeping me company at a restaurant, do you? It's either that or I eat cold spaghetti from a can."

"That's disgusting, Chris. Sounds as if turning you down would be cruel and unusual punishment."

As we drove out of town Chris explained diffidently, "This place we're going to is a little out of the way. I haven't been there before but I hear the food is excellent, almost up to New York standards."

He seemed to be trying to impress me, and I was touched. "Chris," I said, "I don't care about that. A good hamburger or lasagna in town would have been fine."

We took winding roads into the deep countryside, away from the lake and river resorts where the local people usually went for a big night out. We passed through a pretty village I remembered dimly, and then turned down a small road that led into woods where dusk had already fallen. Suddenly there were trimmed evergreens strung with sparkling white lights, a parking lot, a beautiful old stone farmhouse transformed into an inn.

"Chris, it's lovely!"

"Isn't it? My spies were right. Let's see if the food measures up. Susie's been so busy I don't think my stomach remembers real food."

The interior was charming, renovated with gleaming Victorian oak paneling and country wallpaper. The drinks were large and cold and Chris had a second double Scotch while I was finishing my first martini.

"We finally have a chance to talk," Chris said with a satisfied smile. "I want to hear everything you've been doing all these twenty years, Miss Engels, starting with the day after graduation and ending with last week."

As we dug into pasta salad, grilled trout, and a bottle of chablis, I sketched the outlines of my career for Chris. I didn't tell him everything, not even as much as I told Tony, but I hit enough high points to have the satisfaction of seeing that he was impressed.

The conversation eventually did circle back to graduation, and the years before. We laughed a lot, comparing memories of high-school life: the language teacher who insulted lazy students in Latin and then made them translate it; the irreverent young English teacher who told us where our Board of Education-purchased editions of Shakespeare had been censored; the annual fund-raising contest, which pitted boys against girls in a ferociously fought contest that included the faculty and ended in Slave Day, with the losers serving the winners; the Sadie Hawkins dance, when the girls asked the boys, everyone dressed like Li'l Abner and Daisy Mae, and the physics teacher played Marryin' Sam. Chris tried to claim that boys waited in fear beside the phone, praying for a date, just as girls did when the prom approached.

At last I confessed, laughing, "I always wanted to ask you to the Sadie Hawkins dance, but I never had the nerve to even seriously consider it. I had quite a crush on you in those days. Didn't you ever guess?"

"Not for a minute." He shook his head. "Of course I was a young fool. If only I'd known—"

"It would have embarrassed you, that's all," I said quickly. "You wouldn't have done anything about it. My looks were all wrong for a teenager, and I wasn't much fun in those days, either," I went on, saying it aloud for the first time. "I was very unhappy, and it showed. *I* wouldn't have wanted to date me either." I was surprised by what I found myself saying, but it was the truth.

"And look at you now," Chris said with an appreciative smile. "Success suits you."

"Thank you for saying that. It erases a lot of old memories."

"How are your local stories coming along?" Chris asked as he poured more wine. "Will you be here long?"

"For as long as I can stall my boss. He wants me back next week, but there are so many unanswered questions and I hate to leave without answering them. At least I'm beginning to ask the right ones of the right people. I talked to Arthur Langton today. It seems you were wrong about Maggie's will. She left everything to you, Tony, and Terry, split three ways, when you were babies, and she never changed it. Even your own heirs are not included."

"Kay, I'm stunned. I had no idea. She despised Terry and she made it clear I was too much like my father for her to care for me much either. So Tony and I share it all, now that Terry's dead? Of course a half share of almost nothing is still almost nothing. There's no market for an old run-down farm like that. It's hard enough for the best-run farms to make a profit.''

''What about the house?''

''It's a nice house, as I remember it, but it's too far from town for people to commute in the winter. Those back roads get too snowed in. And around here, if someone wants a vacation house, they want it on a beach.''

''So there's no profit at all in being Maggie's heir?''

''Not that I can see. Kay, I don't think there is *any* motive. Forgive me, but I think you and Tony are seeing bogeymen in the shadows. It was an accident and that's all, sad but true.''

''Maybe you're right,'' I admitted with great reluctance, ''but it just doesn't feel right to me. It just doesn't. Anyway, I intend to go on asking questions until I'm absolutely sure one way or another.''

Chris stared at me for a moment with a strange expression, and then said, ''Care for dessert? Or a nightcap?''

''Oh, no. I've had more than enough of both food and alcohol. Just coffee for me.''

''I'll have a nightcap then, but not dessert.'' He asked the waiter for a brandy, then turned back to me. ''What do you think of this place?''

"It's lovely. Good food, too, but isn't it a bit out-of-the-way? How do they manage to attract such a crowd?"

"I have a suspicion," he said, "that a lot of their customers are looking for a really out-of-the-way place where they won't meet any of their neighbors. A place with a few cozy, romantic bedrooms upstairs."

"Oh?"

He nodded. "I've also heard that there's a nice garden out back. Shall we have a look before we leave?"

We were walking in the shadowy garden, Chris's arm draped across my shoulders in a casual, friendly fashion, when all of a sudden the arm tightened, he pulled me close, and his lips were on my ear.

"It's not too late, you know," he whispered. "We could make those teenage daydreams real...you're someone very special...let me make this trip special for you—"

I was so astonished I was speechless. He held me too tight for me to break away, but I leaned back enough to see his face.

Laughter and drink had loosened him up. He looked flushed, untidy, and more relaxed than I had ever seen him, and a little reckless. Not at all the respectable young banker. Very attractive. Very. I had an impulse to put my head on his broad shoulder and just leave it there. To let him go on kissing my ear until he lifted my head to kiss my mouth.

He was looking at my surprised face and laughing. "Oh, come on, Kay. Don't tell me you've never had a married lover, just for the fun of it." Yes, I had, and I swore a long time ago that I would never travel that sad road again.

At last I managed to sputter, "I thought you were such a devoted family man."

"I am. I love Sue, I always will, but Jesus, Kay, we've been together sixteen years and we get a little bored sometimes. Don't pretend to be shocked. You've been around." He pulled me close again, kissing my throat and murmuring, "I could make it so much fun—"

That little exchange had chilled some of the temptation. I said, very distinctly, "Does Sue get bored too?"

"Oh, Sue." He laughed. "She's not the adventurous type."

That was my saving splash of cold water. His smugness so infuriated me that I had no trouble breaking his hold.

"You're drunk. Give me your car keys and I'll drive us both home before we get into trouble."

"I'm drunk? Not too drunk to drive. Sure I can't convince you? Maybe one good kiss would do it. You *know* you feel something." He lunged but I evaded him easily and he stopped.

"Enough games, Kay. You'll regret saying no, but never mind. Here." He tossed me the car keys. "You can drive. I've had a rough day." He smiled unpleasantly. "See if you can find the way home."

I would show him. My sense of direction had served me well in far more exotic and dangerous places than hick upstate New York. I drove fast, furiously, while Chris slumped in the far corner of the front seat, fast asleep. He woke up with a start when I stopped in the hotel parking lot.

"I made a fool of myself, didn't I, Kay? I'm sorry. It's been a hell of a week and too much to drink. Forgive me?"

He was so straightforward, the look in his eyes so genuine, his smile so apologetic, that my anger immediately dissolved.

"I've already forgotten what happened," I assured him, "whatever it was. Go home and sleep it off, Chris. And for God's sake drive carefully."

There was a message waiting for me. It was unsigned, and no one at the desk seemed to know who had brought it. It said, "Go home before you get hurt. This is not a joke."

Oh, hell, I thought. I can't deal with anything else tonight. The note seemed too unreal, written in childish block letters on notebook paper. It seemed like a joke. I would deal with it in the morning.

EIGHTEEN

Saturday morning

IN THE MORNING, the note still seemed like a joke. The
most dangerous people I had encountered by far were
Wishon and his friends, and they were long gone. I
somehow couldn't believe that I had to be afraid of
anyone here. Yes, Terry had been murdered, but I was
sure that had something to do with her tangled life and
nothing to do with me. And I wasn't taking Tony's
suspicions about Maggie that seriously. Maybe the note
was from the older Mr. Campbell, trying to get me to
go away. I had to smile at the picture that created in my
mind: dignified, self-important Mr. Campbell, Esq.,
skulking around leaving anonymous threatening letters. I had more pressing matters to think about.

I called Tony's home and left a message on his answering machine. I called his office but there was no
answer, and I left a message there too. I called the jail
and was told he was out on bail and had left with his
attorney. Frustrated at being unable to tell him what I
had learned from Arthur Langton, I turned back to my
notes from interviews at the hotel. Probably it was a
waste of time, but maybe there was one little thing I
could use. Maybe I just hadn't seen it at first. And
there was. It wasn't much, just a name, Miller Creek

Road, and the possibility that Earl Mayhew lived in a trailer park out there. Why not? I thought. I couldn't seem to do anything else.

Getting into my car, I noticed a battered red pickup truck parked nearby and realized I had been seeing it out of the corner of my eye, on and off, for days. I took another look. Andy. I really was not in the mood for this, and by the time I was rapping on the truck cab's door I was thoroughly exasperated.

"Are you following me around?"

He'd been daydreaming, or half asleep. I startled him.

"Kay! It's great to see you. Would you like to see my truck?"

"No, I would not like to see your truck! I would like to know why you've been following me!"

"Well, I haven't exactly been following you. I just like to be around where you are if I can. I figure sooner or later you'll have some free time, and if I'm right on the spot, we can get together. I'm *never* going to give up."

"Well, I want you to. I'm working, Andy. I'm not here to play, and I have a lot on my mind. I don't want you following me around."

His usually pleasant, vacant face turned dark red. "Now you've made me angry. You'll be sorry. I had something important to tell you, and now I won't. But you'll be really, really sorry you said this to me." He sounded as if he might cry, but he quickly slammed the door and drove away so fast he sprayed gravel.

I hadn't expected that reaction, and it made me wonder if there was more going on in Andy's slow brain than I had realized. Did he send me the note? The handwriting looked right, but the message was all wrong: Andy didn't want me to leave. And was the phone call the day after my encounter with Wishon from Andy, too? Andy, however, was the least important question in my mind that morning, and I forgot about him as soon as I turned to a city map to locate Miller Creek Road.

I found it easily enough, and headed out of town on a street lined with auto repair shops, used car lots, and discount stores. At the city limits the name changed from Center Street to Miller Creek Road and two miles later there was a trailer park. I drove a few miles farther, didn't see another one, and turned back.

Right next to the entrance there was a small, rusted trailer on cement blocks, with a sign that read Office. The inside was as seedy as the outside: worn linoleum floor, a cheap wooden desk, a couple of chairs with peeling paint. There was a rickety card table in the corner on which was set, I was surprised to see, a little pink-and-gold china vase with a fake carnation in it, along with an up-to-date coffee maker, some bright plastic place mats, and a china sugar bowl. I went in and asked the only person there, a worn-out looking woman filing papers, if Earl Mayhew lived there.

"Well," she responded, "yes and no. He lives in that psychedelic van of his. He's got it all painted up inside and out, and carpeted, but of course there's no running water. He parks it here quite a bit, on his friend's trailer site. It's that one, right up there, with the green trailer.'' She pointed without moving. '''Course it's against the rules, but I don't care. It's not here now though, and I haven't seen his friend, name's Buddy, in a couple of days. Why do you want to know?'' she demanded abruptly, as if she'd just realized how unlikely an acquaintance of Earl Mayhew I was. ''He isn't in trouble, is he? 'Cause he's a good kid and I'd tell anyone that. Not real bright, maybe, and not a lot of gumption, but not the troublesome kind at all. That's why I let him stick around.''

''I'd just like to talk to him,'' I said noncommittally. ''Do you have any idea when he'll be back?''

''Not a one. He comes and goes. I could give him a message if I happen to see him.''

''No, thanks. I don't think so.'' I was afraid a message might scare him off. I couldn't believe I was goddamn dead-ended once again.

I turned to leave, then turned back and looked hard across the counter at that graying, overweight, heavy-eyed woman and saw a girl with a reckless smile and pale freckles.

''I *know* you, don't I? And in a minute I'll have your name.''

''It's Betty Lee,'' she said, looking quizzically at me. ''Last name might be Harding, or LaSalle, depending on when you knew me.''

''Or Woodman,'' I said, suddenly remembering. ''You're Betty Lee Woodman, aren't you?''

And I was back in second grade, third grade, fourth grade. Sharing a reader. Sharing an orange popsicle on summer porch steps. Trick-or-treating, holding hands in the spooky October night. Walking to the public pool on hot summer days. And finally losing sight of each other in the bigger world of junior high, and eventually high school. I could not pull up a single memory of Betty after—what?—eighth, ninth, tenth grade?

"I was," she replied, "if you go back far enough." Her frown suddenly cleared. "It's Kay, isn't it? Well, well, a real live ghost. In town for the reunion?"

I nodded. "I didn't see you there."

"I didn't go. Kay, I never even finished high school. You didn't know?"

"I'm sorry. I didn't. We just lost track of each other."

"Of course we did. I never was much of a student. Don't you remember trying to drum the state capitals into me? And I was so boy-crazy, starting in sixth grade, I could have cared less about school or what you were doing or anything. Well, I learned."

"Will you tell me about it?" I asked gently.

"You never heard? Really? And at the time I thought I was the great whore of Falls City! I guess I figured no one in town had anything better to talk about. Not to beat around the bush, I got pregnant in tenth grade and quit school."

"Oh, Betty Lee. I'm so sorry. I never knew. What did you do?"

"My mom stood by me. I think she blamed herself some. You know we went to a real strict gospel church?"

"I remember! When we had square dancing in the gym, you had to sit out."

She nodded. "Right. Couldn't see a movie, neither, not even an educational film at school. And of course I was raised just stone-ignorant about sex, doing everything every chance I got and not knowing one thing about it. And then my minister threw me out of the church 'cause I was a sinner and not quite repentant enough about it," she said bitterly. "Well, I was only fifteen and crazy about the boy. What did he expect? But my mom helped me raise the baby. It was real tough. She'd raised all of us from the time my dad walked out, and there she was with another baby. Of course," Betty added with a mocking smile, "at the time, I was just sorry for myself. I had to grow up some to see it through her eyes. I was on welfare for a while, and that just about broke her heart."

"What about the boy? Who was it anyway?"

"Who? My baby's father? You wouldn't know him. He was from over to Madison Center. He never called or came by once after I told him, though I heard from my girlfriends that he bragged about it all over town." She shook her head. "I'm about off men. I've been married twice, and had a couple of boyfriends in between, and would you believe I never picked a good one yet? I think I'll just be an independent middle-aged cuss."

"Betty Lee, you're only thirty-eight!"

"Oh, hell, Kay, I'm a grandmother twice over. I look middle-aged and Lord knows I feel it."

How could my childhood friend be middle-aged when I so often felt I was still learning how to be a grown-up?

"Well, don't look so shocked. My daughter was just like me, thinking of nothing but boys, but she was smarter. She found a pretty good one and got married at eighteen, *with* her diploma. Got two cute babies. My mom just loves them to death, and so do I." She shrugged, as if to say, "That's my life."

"But you could go on now," I protested. "Go back to school, make a different life."

"What for? Things were awful hard when Debbie was little. I worked all kinds of jobs, sometimes two, just to put food on the table, but now—well, I pretty much run this place. It's not a bad job, get my own trailer plot and hookups free, fixed my trailer up real nice, so my living here doesn't even cost that much. I've got enough to buy my grand-babies a gift every so often and help out my mom, though, God love her," Betty added proudly, "she's still working and won't take much from me."

"If it had happened a few years later," I said thoughtlessly, "your whole life could have been different. I mean after abortion was legal. You could have had an education, a good job, a life." I didn't realize just how thoughtless it was until I saw her face.

"Oh, no, Kay, I could never! Why, Kay, I'm a Christian. I don't believe in that. I mean, I left my old church—I go to the Baptists now—but I could never . . . oh, it was awful hard, but not to have my Debbie . . ."

"Of course," I said hastily, not remotely convinced, but deeply embarrassed. I knew my face was turning red. "I didn't mean . . . I just meant . . ." I made a quick recovery. "Do you have any pictures?"

I admired the heavily made-up daughter with her Farrah Fawcett hairdo in her graduation picture and her wedding picture, and the same girl, thirty pounds heavier but prettier without the makeup, proudly holding two smiling babies in ruffly outfits. Betty asked me about my family, and I answered, "My luck with men has been about the same as yours."

Betty nodded. "I've yet to meet one who's worth the time and energy, over the long haul. I still like to party once in a while, but after, I just want my peace of mind, my own place, my own money. No one to bother about."

"I know what you mean! Sometimes I almost think it's what I want too, but then there are those *other* times—"

Betty smiled. "Oh, I know. Men'll do you in whether you have 'em or you don't. We've just got to do the best with what's handed to us, I suppose."

"It looks to me like you have," I said, and meant it. "It's been good to see you. I can hardly believe it's you."

"It's been good to see you too, Kay. I'll call you if I spot Earl. Just leave me your number. What do you want with him, anyway?"

"It's just to ask him some questions, but Betty, it is really important." My voice shook a little. "I can't say why, but please believe me, and call me right away."

Driving back to town, I hoped as fervently as praying that Earl Mayhew would turn up soon, and that I'd be able to talk to Tony when I got back. I kept thinking about my meeting with Betty, and then something she said came back to me vividly. She'd mentioned her minister, and how he'd let her down when she became pregnant.

We had a minister too. Everyone did, because everyone in town went to church, it seemed. It was Reverend Schulz, and he was a kind, soft-spoken, youngish man when I was growing up. And my mother was close to him, thought highly of him, and relied on his advice. Maybe, just maybe, he knew something about me. If he was still in town. If I could reach him. If he remembered us after all these years.

I looked at the phone book as soon as I got back. No. No Schulzes at all. Maybe he was dead, but maybe he had just transferred to another town, or retired. I called the church and got lucky. He was retired, and lived in a little village nearby, out in the country. They gave me his number.

When his voice, older sounding but familiar, came on the line my heart was beating so fast I could hardly breathe.

"Reverend Schulz? This is Kay Engels. I don't know if you remember me? My parents belonged to Main Street Methodist when I was a girl, in the fifties and sixties."

There was a pause on the other end, and then he said, "Kay Engels! Of course I remember you! It just took my old brain a moment. You were one of the best Sunday School pupils I ever had. And your parents were such fine people, and so proud of you. How are they?"

It was my turn to pause. "They died, Reverend. Many years ago."

"I am sorry to hear that. I would have written to you if I'd known, but you know, like so many people, once they made the decision to uproot themselves and move to Florida, they really did pull up all the roots and never looked back. And how are you? Where do you live now?"

"I live in New York, but actually I'm in town now, and I was wondering if you might...if you would...be able to help me with...with something...a problem...?" My heart was no longer pounding too fast in my chest. It was entirely in my mouth.

"I'd be happy to help, if I can," he responded promptly. "Being a minister's a lifetime job. You don't really retire. What can I do for you?"

"This is...it's very strange...but did my mother...did she ever tell you about me?"

"Often. I heard about every school prize, every report card."

"No, I don't mean that." I took a deep breath. "Did she ever tell you about my being adopted?"

"Yes, Kay," he said, very gently. "We talked about it just once. She was uneasy about not having told you, and she came to me for advice."

I couldn't believe my ears. I wanted to dance, I was so excited.

"She never did tell me. I only learned about it by accident, this week. Please tell me about it. I may not be able to find out any other way."

"Kay, I'm so sorry. I can't. I don't know anything."

"But you must, if she talked to you—" No, I was thinking. No. I must have misunderstood what he said.

"She wouldn't tell me any of the background at all. All I ever knew was that you were adopted, and that you'd never been told. It was very difficult to advise her without knowing more than that, and I told her so, but she was adamant about it. In the end, all I could say was that she had to follow her own conscience. I'm sure she did. She was a good woman."

"Yes." I could barely get the words out. "Yes. I guess so. Thanks for talking to me. I have to . . . I think I have to go now."

"I understand. But Kay, if you'd like to talk, come by anytime. It would be a real pleasure for Mrs. Schulz and me to see you."

"Thank you. I . . . thanks. Good-bye."

I sat there on the edge of my hotel bed, furious and disappointed, for a long time. How could they have done this to me? Every argument we'd ever had, every grievance I'd felt in the stormy years of my adolescence, came back to me—and none of them could compare to this. Sue had said it was cruel to keep a child and mother apart. By their silence, that's exactly what they had done. Maybe there were answers in that old box of papers, but I doubted it. It would have been just like them to destroy anything that would now tell me what I wanted to know. I began to realize that I might have to accept Campbell's offer or never know the answers. How could I do that? And how could I not do it?

I sat there thinking, my thoughts racing around and around until my head ached with questions. I had to escape from all these personal questions, and, as always, work was the best answer. I took two aspirin and tried unsuccessfully to reach Tony. I told myself, more than once, that he was undoubtedly okay. Knowing there was nothing more to do about Maggie's death and dead-ended, at least for now, on Earl Mayhew, I decided to follow up on another thread and see if I could talk to Laurie McDowell.

It was Saturday, so she wouldn't be at school, and the Y told me she wasn't scheduled for any classes that day. I hoped I would finally get lucky with something and surprise her at her house.

NINETEEN

THE MCDOWELL'S HOUSE was a neatly kept, shingled Cape Cod in a neighborhood of identical small houses, put up in a hurry right after World War II and long since individualized by added rooms, tacked-on bay windows, punched-through skylights, and a vast variety of fence styles. The McDowells' was traditional white picket, with climbing roses. The house was white too, with green-shuttered windows on either side of the green door, two sweet little white benches in front, and a rose-bordered flagstone walk. It was just like a child's picture of a pretty house.

There was a police car parked in the driveway. I pushed the doorbell and kept pushing until Laurie, looking flustered and annoyed, came to the door.

"Hi, Laurie," I said with a pleasant smile, "I just stopped by on an impulse, hoping we could talk now."

"I'm busy," she said, immediately trying to close the door.

"I think you ought to make the time," I said, still pleasantly but in a louder voice.

As I was hoping, this provoked an answer from within. Chief LaForge's voice called out, "Laurie, is it that reporter woman? Tell her to butt out. This is your private home, and we're in a criminal investigation here. Do I have to throw her out?"

"Oh, no, chief," I said. Taking advantage of Laurie's confusion, I stepped quickly into the house and leaned against the living room door frame, a picture, I hoped, of perfect self-possession and reasonableness.

"Oh, no," I repeated. "I think you need me here. I know some things you're probably telling Laurie, and she ought to hear them directly from me. Don't you think so, Laurie?"

"Oh, I don't know! Yes, I guess so. I'm sorry, Uncle Al. I don't know what to do about anything right now but I guess I'd like to hear what she has to say too. I might just as well hear it all."

I took a seat and the chief, though obviously furious at being trapped, gave in and didn't order me to leave.

"Look, honey," he said to Laurie with awkward gentleness, "we just need to ask you some questions about the night of the reunion. Some things came up." He glanced at me and then quickly looked away again. "Some things came up and there are just these... questions. You know I'm not going to let you say anything that will get you into trouble, and if you are already in trouble, you know I'll do my best for you. But you've got to talk to me. Isn't it better here, friendly, than in my office?"

"Yes," Laurie said grimly, looking up at last from the hands clenched in her lap. She looked straight at him and said, "I'm ready."

"We need to know where you were during the re-union. Did you leave the room for a while? Try your best to remember the whole evening."

"I went out to the ladies room a few times. I walked in the hall with friends when we wanted a quieter place to talk. I don't remember anything else." She stopped and closed her mouth abruptly, as if deliberately stopping herself from saying whatever else there was to say.

"Honey, did you wear a bow in your hair at the party? Some fancy thing?"

"Yes, on a comb, with flowers on it. What in the world?...Oh," she said, turning pale. "I lost it somewhere."

"Since you've managed to be here," the chief said to me, "against my wishes, you might as well tell her what you told me."

"A maid asked me if I lost it, Laurie. She found it in the hall right outside my room and Terry's."

"This is serious, Laurie. You've got to tell us how you happened to lose it right there."

Laurie couldn't seem to meet his sympathetic eyes. She looked at me, around the room, and finally back at her hands in her lap.

"I'm so ashamed," she whispered. "I went to see if Richie was there. I don't know what I would have done. I guess I just finally wanted to know *for sure*, though I guess I really did know, deep down, anyway. They've been having an affair for years. I guess I had some crazy idea that if I found them together, he'd be so ashamed. Or maybe if she was alone, and I begged her."

A key turned in the front door and we heard Richie's voice before we saw him.

"Laurie? I'm home. Is everything all right? Angie called to say she saw the police car and..." His voice faltered when he saw all of us in the living room, but then he went on, "and I was afraid there might be something wrong."

"Police cars have been in the driveway before and busybody Angie always calls you," Laurie said. "I've got a godfather and a cousin on the force. You never came home before. Just what did you think might be wrong this time?"

"Well, I don't know," Richie stammered, taken aback. "I thought—"

"Sit down and shut up," the chief said quietly. "Laurie has some important things to tell us. It'll do you a world of good to hear them. Go on, Laurie. You were in front of Terry's room that night—"

"You were *what*?"

"Shut up, I said," LaForge snapped. "Now go on, honey. Did you hear anything?"

She shook her head. "It was so quiet, I didn't know what to do. Finally, I thought and thought about them together, and I got so angry I tried the door. It wasn't even locked. I don't know what I thought I was going to do, or what I was capable of, but I saw her lying on the bed, and I hated her so much," Laurie said, her voice shaking, "I think I could have killed her then and there, but—" she gasped and started crying, "she was already dead."

I looked up quickly to meet the chief's eyes. Handing her his big handkerchief, he asked, "Do you happen to have any idea what time that was?"

She nodded, wiping her eyes. "I know," she said, sobbing, "because when I leaned over her to see if she was asleep, I saw a gold watch on the table just exactly like the one Richie gave me for our fifteenth anniversary. And I looked at it. I couldn't help myself." She turned to look directly at her husband for the first time. "It said on the back, 'Love always. Rich,' just like mine. How *could* you?"

He tried to say something, but I couldn't wait. "Laurie, what time was it?"

She closed her eyes. "I can still see it. Eleven-forty-five."

I barely managed to suppress my stunningly inappropriate smile. "That clears Tony. I don't care what that kid Mayhew told you. At eleven-forty-five Tony was dancing with me. I know, because the bandleader said something about it coming on toward midnight and a special number for the witching hour. Probably dozens of other people could tell you he was there."

The chief nodded. He heard, but his attention was devoted to Laurie, sobbing on his shoulder.

"It's all right now, it's all right. It's okay now." He patted her shoulder, but his face was troubled. I could hear his questions just as clearly as if he were asking them out loud. "How do I know if she's telling the truth? And how do I prove it? And if she isn't, how can I bear to prove that? And how do I face myself every day if I don't?" He looked like an old man for the first time since I'd met him.

Laurie looked up at last and said to all of us, "I'm glad she's dead. Glad! I didn't do it, but I think I could have, and I'd like to thank the person who did."

"Laurie, you don't mean that!" Richie blurted.

"Don't I?" she said with a sad smile. "You know, we could have been happy. I never looked at anyone but you, and I know I could have made you love me the same way, but she was some kind of goddess to you. Even in high school you dropped me every time she waved her hand at you. I thought *she* finally dropped *you* for good when she married someone richer, and then we could be happy together, but every time she came to town it would start all over again. She'd just wiggle her fingers, or her behind, and you'd be right back in her hands, and her mouth, and her bed."

"Laurie, you never talked like that!"

"Oh, shut up, Richie," she said wearily. "I can talk dirty if I want to. Bet you didn't mind when she did it. You really thought I didn't know, didn't you? All these years? All those mysterious errands whenever she was in town?"

"And then I'd run into her somewhere and she'd talk girl talk to me, like we were friends or something. 'Oh, Laurie, your husband is so handsome.' 'He was such a great date in high school. Clever girl to steal him from me!' 'He has such great shoulders. And great legs.'

Then she'd look at me with those cool, cool eyes and grin, and watch me think about her hands on your shoulders and her legs wrapped around yours." Laurie was breathing hard, her hands clenched into two tight little fists on her lap. "You fool. Did you think you were the only one? Her great love? She was just playing games. And you wrecked my life, and yours, for it. And she wrecked plenty of others too, I bet. She had it coming and I'm glad someone did it!"

Then she started crying hysterically, shaking off LaForge's attempts at comfort.

"Oh, go away, all of you. I'm humiliated enough. Just leave me alone."

LaForge and I moved silently toward the door, but he stopped to grip Richie's arm so hard he left white finger marks on the suntanned skin. He whispered, "Neglect her now and I'll kill you. And if you don't spend the rest of your life making it up to her, you'll wish you were dead. One wrong step, just one. Do you read me?"

Richie, speechless, swallowed hard and nodded, and then the chief and I left together.

Outside, he said, "You're sure about the time you were with Campbell? You'd swear to it? Oh, hell, guess we'll have to drop the charges. I never was really convinced, but we had that witness. I should have known it was too good to be true. Now I'll have to track him down again and ask a whole lot more questions. Oh, hell."

Then he turned to me. "Enjoyed that, did you? Bet that'll give a nice dramatic touch to your story. God, how do you live with yourself?"

Stung, I answered, "No, I did not enjoy it." Even as I said it, though, I knew that I would remember everything I had witnessed, and that I would surely use it if it made a better story. I was a little ashamed, but I went on, furiously, "And I live with myself the same way you will, if there's any more evidence pointing to her. You're doing your job in the best way you know how, and so am I.

"My job is to tell the truth no matter who doesn't want me to, and I'm damn good at it. It's the most important thing in my life, and the most honest, and the only thing I do right. It's who I am, and if you don't want me to do it, you can go to hell!" And I knew I wasn't saying that just to him.

"I don't want someone I love to get hurt. That's all." He walked back to his car with the bent back of an old man, and drove away.

I sat in mine for a while, staring at that neat, sweet little house and thinking it should look more like a pile of rubble, the way places usually look after a bomb goes off.

I drove away slowly until I found myself in front of the building that housed Tony's office, as well as Arthur Langton's. Across the street was a large old house converted into offices, with a sign in front that read William Campbell, Esquire, Attorney. I realized that somewhere in my mind, all along, I'd been planning to find Tony, but first I had something to say, right now, to Mr. Campbell. Lots of small-town professional men keep Saturday hours. Hoping, I rang the bell.

He opened the door himself. "You're lucky to find me in now that I'm semiretired, but with all these family tragedies, I have a great deal of business to attend to."

He sat down behind his big mahogany desk and motioned me to an old-fashioned high-backed brown leather chair.

"I presume you've come to tell me you're going to be sensible and accept my offer."

"No, Mr. Campbell, I haven't," I said, concentrating hard on keeping my voice very firm. I would never let him know how I really felt. "You have something I want, and I want it very badly, but I already have something I need more, and that's my work. I just told someone that it's the best and most important thing in my life, and it is. I can't sell it out for anything you can offer me. I just can't."

"Why, Miss Engels," he said with a slight bow of his head and an ironic smile, "you're talking about professional ethics. How interesting that even reporters think they have some."

I nodded.

"A useful concept, professional ethics, but it's foolish to let such an abstraction get in the way of one's life. Without my files, you'll never know who you are."

I knew that. I knew it, and it hurt, and I hated him for pointing it out, but I gave him my best answer and, saying it, I knew it was the truth.

"I already know who I am. I'm a reporter. What I don't know is who my parents were, and I'd like to, but it's not worth it if the price is giving up who I already am. I'll have to find another way, or learn to live without knowing."

I got up to leave. Pride and anger had carried me through so far, but I didn't know how much longer they would. My knees and my will were both starting to give way.

"You're making a real mistake. We could have done this amicably, but I want you to know that if you drag our family onto the pages of that scandal sheet, we'll sue you for decades—millions—"

I walked out and went straight to Tony's office, longing for a friendly face.

His secretary was there. A cheerful older woman, she told me she was taking advantage of a quiet Saturday to catch up on overdue paperwork. Tony had been in to pick up his mail but had gone out again, probably for the rest of the day. She didn't know where he could be reached. Leaving the building, I met Langton in the vestibule.

"I'm available for a late lunch," he said. "It would be an honor to have a lovely young lady such as yourself join me."

I realized quite suddenly that I was famished. I wasn't really anxious for company, but I was touched and flattered, and somewhat at a loss as to what would be my most useful next move. We went across the street to his club, a comfortably shabby place where the motherly waitresses knew everyone by name and served homey, old-fashioned food.

So this was the great, exclusive Falls City Club, a place I never expected to set foot in. I know my parents never did in their entire lifetimes in Falls City. I compared it momentarily to the imposing clubs where I had dined in New York and Washington, with members any newspaper reader in America would recognize, and then I dismissed the thought. Mr. Langton was amusing and charming, as if making up for his maudlin behavior the day before, and I was determined to be the same.

He recommended the macaroni and cheese—freshly made with sharp local cheddar—and cherry cobbler. It was all surprisingly delicious. Over lunch he gossiped about the people in the room and told scandalous stories about the club's earlier and rowdier days, and I actually enjoyed myself immensely.

As he signed for the lunch and guided me to the coat room I said, "By the way, I saw Chris yesterday, and we talked a little about Maggie's will. What you told me came as quite a surprise to him."

The old man stopped and stared at me. "Did it?" he said. "Now that's a surprise to me. I don't believe Tony ever knew, because he was still in New York, but Chris was there, certainly. He must have forgotten."

"Forgotten what?" I tried hard to say it patiently.

"Sorry, my dear. Losing the thread of my conversation here. Some years ago Maggie had a spell of serious illness, and her brothers came to see me, and brought Chris too, because he's here year-round and they wouldn't be when they retired. They wanted to make arrangements for her property, bank accounts and so on, just in case, you know. I had her permission to lay it all out for them. So Chris did know. As I said, he must have forgotten. It's not just us old folks who do that, you know."

Later, I began to wonder if Chris had really forgotten. I didn't think it was the sort of thing a banker forgets. He seemed to be trying so hard to convince me that the land was valueless, too. Too hard? Or had his behavior the other night made me start seeing shadows where there were none?

The time had come for some old-fashioned, hardcopy research. I spent what was left of the afternoon at the public library studying country maps and at the newspaper reading the entire fat file on the county's biggest story, the ongoing expansion of Fort Oake. Then I returned to my room to make what had to be a very private phone call.

TWENTY

I COULDN'T BELIEVE IT. I was trying to call an old boyfriend at the Department of Defense and he wasn't there. How could he not be there when I needed to talk to him so badly? Of course it was Saturday, but he was the type who always let someone know where he could be reached in case of a problem. After some pushing from me, the operator admitted that he was at an official reception and that she could probably locate him, but only in the case of an official emergency. She was not too impressed with my all-too-civilian credentials, knew that I was not his wife, and refused to contact him for me. She refused to contact an officer who could release any information to me. She refused to give me any information at all except the offensively obnoxious advice that I could call back on Monday. She would not even tell me what time he was expected in. She admitted, reluctantly, that she could relay my message to him and he could call me. Maybe.

Of course there was no answer when I called him at home. Of course. He had already left for that reception. I slammed the phone down and cursed loudly and at length. Dead-ended again, just when I was finally beginning to have a suggestion of a glimpse of an idea.

Tony had called twice but hadn't left more than his name. He wasn't at his home or office and there was no one else in town I wanted to see. I didn't want to go out anyway, in case he called, or Betty did, or my army friend did, and I resigned myself to a lonely evening in my room. I had dinner with a newspaper in the dining room, leaving instructions to have me paged if I got a call. I returned and tried to work, but couldn't seem to concentrate. I was dismayed and depressed that the professional self-discipline I had cultivated for so many years was fraying so rapidly and completely.

I had books I didn't want to read, a television I didn't want to watch, and a comfortable room I didn't want to be in and didn't want to leave. My bruised jaw still hurt whenever I stopped to think about it, and I seemed to be unusually exhausted. My work wasn't progressing. I didn't know enough to work on my plans for my book. I finally gave it all up, including the effort to think, and turned on an excruciatingly silly TV movie.

The next thing I was aware of was a man's voice. My brain seemed to be covered by a fuzzy blanket. I slowly realized I had been asleep. A man's voice? Was someone in the room? I snapped awake but cautiously kept my eyes closed. Totally alert now, I listened hard for footsteps. Could I figure out where he was before he knew I was awake?

"Let us strive to continue in God's path..."

It was Oral Roberts conducting a Sunday morning service. I'd fallen asleep with the TV on, and yes, fully clothed and on top of the bedspread. No wonder I didn't feel rested.

I checked the clock. Almost eight. I could try the Pentagon again soon. No, it was Sunday. I could call him at home. I'd better have some cold water on my face and hot coffee inside me before I did. As soon as I felt prepared I dialed Washington. He was there this time, and answered himself.

"Kay! It's great to hear from you. What do you want?"

"Sam, why are you so sure I want something?"

"'Cause that's the only time you ever call," he replied promptly.

I laughed. "Seems to me I used to say that about you, way back when."

"Ah, but it wasn't information I wanted," he said warmly. "And that's not true anyway. We had some great times. Do you remember—"

"I know we did, Sam," I cut in, "and now you're a happily married man with two lovely kids, and I do want some information."

"I knew it," he said. "Fire away."

When I was done, he asked, "Is it important?"

I answered, "I don't know yet. It might be, it might be truly a matter of life and death."

"Okay. I actually know the guy who should be handling this, and if he's not there I can probably take a look at his files. Fortunately I outrank him. Let me see if I can catch him now at home. Sit tight and I'll try to get back to you some time this morning."

I rearranged my notes, rearranged my clothes, memorized the room-service menu and my airline schedule. I watched the clock. When the phone rang I had it off the hook before it completed the first ring.

"I've got it, Kay. Ready?"

I wrote rapidly as he spoke, excited that my guesses seemed to have been confirmed.

"So that's it. Is it a help?"

"More than you'll ever know. Sam, you're an angel!"

"Damn right. I always was. You just didn't recognize it," he laughed. "But listen, I want a copy of the whole story when you write it, and just one other thing—"

"I know, I know, leave your name out of it."

"Of course. Oh, and I almost forgot something funny. The guy I was talking to said someone else had just lately been asking him the same questions, an old college buddy of his who was in town."

"Do you by any chance have the name?"

"Of course I do. I've got it here somewhere. Just a minute. Here it is, Chris Campbell. Mean anything to you?"

I gasped; told Sam I loved him, sent my best to Kitty and the kids, and said good-bye. I stared at my notes for a long time, trying to see how the pieces fit together. It was still just a collection of very odd facts, with not nearly enough in between to take to the police, but I began to type furiously. The computer screen would be what a sheet of paper had been throughout my life, my confidant and best friend. Put into words the muddled would become clear, the hidden obvious.

When I was done, everything I knew so far was written down and organized. Unfortunately, I still couldn't see just how the pieces of the puzzle fit together, but I was sure now that they did.

I jumped when the phone rang.

"Kay! Finally. Where have you been?" It was Tony at last.

"All over, and I'm full of news. I could ask you the same question, by the way."

"I'd answer it the same way too." I could hear the smile in his voice. My sharp tone seemed to amuse him. "At home to wash off my night in jail; at Maggie's; at church, arranging her funeral. I'll be visiting some anxious clients this afternoon. We've got a lot to talk about. How about dinner? Seven-thirty?"

"Yes. Great. See you then."

I couldn't help smiling as I put the phone down. Suddenly, I'd had enough of everything: my room, my work, mysteries, everything. I'd done all I could for now. I announced defiantly to my whip-cracking inner self that I was taking a break, and that was that.

I tossed a bathing suit and towel into the car, bought a beer, an Italian sub sandwich, and vinegar-flavored potato chips—a delicacy then available only near the border, where stores cater to Canadian tourists' tastes—and headed for the beach.

I had a choice of beaches. The lake shore was ringed with well-kept and empty state parks. I could drive down along the shore about twenty miles to a wide, grassy beach, with dunes that looked out onto an empty vista of sky and water. I used to think that's what the ocean would be like and I wasn't far wrong. I could go to the nearest beach, a fast fifteen minutes away, where the view was of peninsulas and harbors and a land mass that I still couldn't identify as an island or Canada. Or I could go to the park on one of the Thousand Islands, where the beach was small, the view spectacular, and the water the paralyzingly icy St. Lawrence River.

I opted for the nearest beach. I'd forgotten how pleasant it really was, with picnic tables scattered on the grass under the trees and a long, narrow strip of sand rimming the shore. I could remember when the shore was all slippery gray rocks and getting into water deep enough to swim meant risking stubbed toes, cut feet, and painful falls. Each summer the sand strip seemed to grow a little bigger and extended a little farther underwater, until it was possible to walk comfortably all the way to the ropes that marked the limits of the swimming area. When I was a child I just assumed that helpful nature was taking the rocks away. Now of course I realized it was the State Park Commission and many hours of backbreaking labor for someone.

On this beautiful summer Sunday there were plenty of people at the beach: family groups of all ages and sizes; a noisy crowd of children under a big banner that said, "Mt. Olive Vacation Bible School"; teenagers in raucous gangs or as couples who seemed to spend hours rubbing suntan lotion on each other; and groups of lonely looking young men with dog tags around their necks, presumably soldiers from the base. Yet compared to the beaches I usually went to in New York and at fashionable vacation spots, it seemed spacious and quiet.

I swam in the shallow water, warm after two months of summer sun, and ate my deliciously indigestible sandwich while magazines lay in the sand unread. I let the sun bake some of my mood out of me as I lay there looking at families with young children and remembering trips to the beach when I was a very little girl.

I hadn't thought of that part of my childhood in such a long time. Whenever I thought of my parents over the years, which was seldom, I remembered my difficult adolescence and the few years afterward before they died, when the gulf between us became unbridgeable. When I stopped being a nice girl because I wore miniskirts and pierced my ears. When I became a snob because I couldn't stand evening after evening of nothing but watching TV and eating chips. When I put my soul in jeopardy by refusing to go to church. When I couldn't wait to return to college in a big, bad city where I might be exposed to all kinds of radicals and degenerates. I used to tell them that's exactly why I was going.

Now my mind went further back. I started remembering trips to the beach with them, sometimes right after they returned from work, to have a cool supper in those days when air-conditioning was still an expensive luxury. My father would teach me to swim in the warm, still water of early evening, and I would stay in until the sky was turning dark and my lips were blue. My mother made elaborate picnics, with deviled eggs and homemade potato salad and fresh-picked watermelon bought at a roadside stand on the way out. And a frosted chocolate layer cake in its own special carrier.

Birthday cakes that she made for me, decorated with circus animals or elaborately dressed kewpie dolls. Birthday parties with chocolate-vanilla-strawberry ice cream and little frilled crepe-paper cups to hold the candy, and me in a frilled dress to match.

Christmas, with each year's most heavily advertised doll always under the overdecorated artificial tree, and a new red dress. I seemed to remember embroidered holly leaves on a few of them.

They were people who never read a thing but *Reader's Digest*, yet they took me to the library every week when my teachers said they should. They were people who knew no more about music than what they heard on *Your Hit Parade*, yet they sent me for piano lessons when the choir leader said I had a good ear.

As I lay in the sun half dreaming it came to me, perhaps for the first time, that maybe they'd done the best they could. How baffled, and eventually hurt, they'd been when I wanted books instead of dolls, black turtlenecks instead of pretty ruffled blouses, Bach instead of Connie Francis, and ultimately algebra and French and college instead of a secretarial course. I knew I hadn't stopped at rejecting what they'd liked; I'd made fun of it.

But if I'd needed much more from life than they could give or plan for or even understand, they didn't really stand in my way. After all the fighting and all the hurt silences they'd helped me get off to college, bought me luggage, sent me cookies. They'd done the best they could. I'd been sad when they died, just a few months apart, my last year in college, but I hadn't really missed them much. For the first time in my life, I wished they'd lived until I'd grown up a bit more. I wasn't ready to give up finding my biological mother, but I had to admit to myself that I knew who my real parents were.

Then I must have dozed, because the next time I looked the sun was lower. My skin was warm and still smelled of sunlight, but the air was cool. I shivered suddenly. It was time to go.

I could smell charcoal and meat barbecuing as families started their suppers, and I heard parents calling their children, "Lauren, get out of the water right now!" "Come on, Abby, off the swings and out of that wet suit." "Matt, give me a hand here." "Sally, it's suppertime. Come on."

I used to know a Sally, I thought dreamily. Of course I did. I sat right up. My mother's cousin Sally. I could still remember meeting her only once, when I was quite small. I have just a dim memory of bright lipstick, sweet perfume, and sparkly earrings. Every once in a while she would send me a wonderful present, something my parents never would have thought of buying or perhaps could not have afforded: a spectacular kaleidoscope, an *Arabian Nights* illustrated with gorgeous full-color plates, a gold-link bracelet with a tiny working music box as a charm.

I must have asked about her when I was young, but my mother was good at answering questions without saying anything. Was I remembering responses, or making them up? "Oh, she lives far away... never really were very close... not one for letters..."

The presents grew less frequent so gradually that I never noticed when they stopped for good. Cousin Sally had simply faded from my mind.

I wondered now if my mother had continued a once-a-year exchange of Christmas cards. Was Sally still alive? Even an old address book of my mother's would be a start. I'd have to get those boxes out of storage. I could hire a detective. I'd even met a few, working on various stories. As I stood up and brushed the sand from my legs I promised myself that if there was anything at all to go on, no matter how small, I would make the most of it.

I wanted to wash the sand out of my hair before my date, but I never got the chance. The phone was ringing when I walked into the room.

"Tony?"

"Kay? No, it's Betty. Earl just pulled into the park. You said to call."

"I'll be right out. Can you do something to keep him there?"

"Oh, sure, I'll offer him dinner. Never fails. Come to my trailer, second one in, dark red with petunias in the window boxes."

"You're terrific. I'm on my way."

I left a message for Tony on his machine and flew through the streets, hitting the city limits doing sixty. I was out at Miller Creek Road in ten minutes and knocking on Betty's door in twelve.

Betty introduced me to Earl as an old friend and offered me a beer, and I joined them at the tiny dinette table. Earl Mayhew turned out to be a skinny kid in jeans, with greasy, longish hair and a straggly, pathetic mustache. He acknowledged Betty's introduction with a half-smile and a nod and then turned his attention back to his food. I waited only a few minutes before saying directly to him, "Why did you lie about seeing Tony Campbell in Terry's room the night she was killed?"

He choked on his pork and beans, turned red, then jumped up and looked around wildly, as if trying to find an escape. When he saw that he was trapped in the tiny trailer dining area he sat down again, protesting incoherently.

"Earl," I said firmly, "I know you lied, and I believe Chief LaForge does too. He's bound to find you any time now. Don't you know that's obstructing justice, maybe perjury? I want to know why, and if you tell me, I'll try to help you get out of the big, big trouble you're in."

Breathing hard, the boy stammered, "He said he'd take my van, I'd never get it back . . . or even ever get a car loan. It's my best thing, a man needs a set of wheels. . . ."

"Not Tony. Who?"

"No, not him. I can't tell you." The boy was almost sobbing. "He said . . . if I did what he told me to . . . he'd wipe out my overdue payments . . . he could do that . . . but I could never tell anyone . . . never . . . never tell . . ."

"Chris. It was Chris Campbell. My God."

Earl nodded at last. "I didn't tell, did I? You guessed, right? I didn't mean to do anything real bad. I didn't know, at first, it was about a murder. And then I was scared. I didn't want to lose my van."

"But Earl, don't you realize you could go to jail for this?" I said it sympathetically. Some of that sympathy was even genuine. "You'd like to tell now, wouldn't you? That way Chief LaForge won't be so mad at you. He might even call you a good citizen for coming forward, instead of sending you to jail. Why don't you call him? Would you like me to call him for you?" Mayhew nodded and Betty pointed me to the phone.

I left when Earl had finished talking to the chief. An officer was coming out to pick him up and Betty assured him repeatedly that she'd stick by him. I needed to be alone. I had to think.

I drove quickly but thought slowly, carefully. The answers were finally coming together. I could just about fill in the 'who,' 'when,' and 'how' of both murders, and even what he might have gained, but the 'why' was still a blank sheet of paper. Why was what he gained important enough to kill for it? Without that question answered, I could not, would not, believe the rest.

TWENTY-ONE

As I WALKED from the parking lot to my room, a hand grabbed my arm tightly, and someone whispered, "Keep quiet." I was pulled away from the late summer sun and into the long twilight shadows under the trees.

It was Chris.

"I want you to come with me, right now."

"I'm not going anywhere with you, Chris. I have plans and I'm going to my room to get ready. Now let me go." I made myself sound a lot calmer than I felt and I was thinking fast. "Tony's picking me up any minute."

"No, he's not, and you *are* coming with me." There was a gun in his hand.

He held my arm very tightly as he led me to his car. It hurt. Anyone happening to be in the parking lot would see only an affectionate couple.

In the car he buckled me into the seat and tied my hands to the arm rests.

I sat still, since I had no other choice, and tried to think clearly. Chris didn't look villainous. He looked haggard and unhappy.

"I've known you since I was in seventh grade," I thought to myself, looking at him sideways. "I was a head taller than you then. I remember you rocking out at dances in the gym, and dropping your notes during a student council election speech, and yelling so hard at a basketball game you couldn't talk in class the next day. How can I believe this is real? And how can I be afraid of you?''

But I knew the gun was in his pocket, and I was afraid.

I've been in worse spots, I said to myself, clenching my fists so he couldn't see my shaking hands. Every day in Beirut was worse. I can handle this. I know I can. I can, if I can just keep my head. If I can just think clearly.

''Chris,'' I said, struggling to sound matter-of-fact, ''what are you trying to do?''

''We're going to Tony's cottage. You and I are going for a little sailboat ride.''

''At this hour? It will be dark soon.''

''Kay, it's not a pleasure trip. You're in my way, I've made plans and I'll do what I have to do to make them work.'' He paused, swallowed hard, went on. ''You're not coming back. When someone finds the boat in a day or two, wrecked on a small island, you'll be dead and all the evidence will point to Tony. The gun in my pocket is his, by the way.''

''Tony is with his lawyer tonight. I know it for a fact,'' I lied. ''It won't work. He has an alibi.''

Chris was grinning as we approached Tony's cottage. ''I know his lawyer went back to New York. And I thought you were meeting Tony? Anyway, it doesn't matter. I took care of that. I gave him a message from you, telling him you wanted to meet him at a private beach he and I both know. I said it was about Maggie. The beach is closed for work now. No one's there. He'll never be able to prove he wasn't here, and no one knows I am. You see, I'm even parking here on the road so I won't leave tire marks in the dirt driveway."

Even before he pushed the gearshift into park I began begging him to untie me quickly. "The rope hurts so much. Please, Chris!" His words were tough, but his face wasn't. Not at all. If I could reach that part of him, I had a little plan. Not a great one, but better than none. I promised, "I won't do anything. I'm too afraid of that gun."

"All right, all right. Just be quiet while I get this knot." I watched, waiting for the moment when my hands would be free while he was still behind the wheel, putting out the lights, turning off the ignition. I flipped the door handle and hit the ground running, speeding toward the shelter of the house, but he was faster than I expected. I was tackled around the waist and landed on the grass with a punishing, breathtaking crash. His hand gripped mine until I thought it would break and then I felt the gun in my ribs.

"Dumb, Kay. I never expected dumbness from you. You've got nowhere to go. Don't make it harder than it has to be. Move."

"If you're going to kill me anyway, why not tell me the whole story?"

"I don't believe you! You've got a gun in your ribs and you still can't stop asking questions." He hesitated, then said, "Sure. Why not? It's the least I can do, give you your story, even if you'll never get to write it." He waved the gun at Tony's picnic table. "Have a seat, but don't try to run again." He sat at the end of the bench, still pointing the gun at me. "You've already got it figured out anyway, don't you?"

"I guess so. Most of it. It has to do with Maggie's land doesn't it? It's about to become very valuable. The army has a deal with a private builder to put up service family housing, and they're going to buy a chunk of land that includes all of Maggie's farm. No one knows it yet, and no one's guessed, because it's not that close to the base, but there are some other issues, politics, land use, I don't know exactly, and that's where they decided to build. You found out by luck, I think. You have an old friend at the Pentagon."

Chris nodded. "We went to school together; then he became a career officer. I was down in D.C. on business, we had dinner, he just mentioned he was involved with the plans for Oake, said he might even surprise me with a visit sometime. He never was a great brain. A few drinks and the right questions and I knew everything."

"And you and Terry and Tony would someday inherit Maggie's farm. You knew that. And the army's money split three ways wasn't much, but all of it in one pocket made a tidy sum. So you murdered Terry and then Maggie. What about Tony?" He just looked at me. "Oh. He was supposed to go to jail for murdering Terry and now he's going for murdering me."

"That's it, more or less. Clever girl. I tried to scare you off with a threatening message. Amateurish, wasn't it? Then I tried to keep you from it by distracting you."

"You mean the other night?"

He nodded. "I didn't want to do it this way. I really didn't. I thought if I could get you involved with me, you'd stop asking those questions. This wouldn't be happening now if you had gone along."

The lights from the car were bright enough for me to see that he was looking at me with an expression of reproach.

"It wouldn't have been a chore to go through with it, but I don't play around. I really am a family man."

"Then why the hell are you doing this?"

"For them. Until a year ago I was just what everyone thinks I am. Really. Do you believe me?"

I nodded, my eyes on the gun.

"But then I, well, I screwed up. I made some real dumb financial moves, and then I followed up with some more. Me, the successful young banker. I couldn't face Sue with it."

"That bad?"

"That bad, and worse. I lost a lot of money. A lot. I was so sure I could make it back that I..." I saw him look away from my eyes, and the gun tremble, but only for a moment. "I helped myself to money that didn't belong to me. It was stupid. I know it. I thought I could just put it back before I had to account for it, and then I'd come clean to Sue about the rest. But there was no way I could find to do it until all of a sudden a way opened up, in Washington.''

Appalled but fascinated, I had to go on asking questions. "So that's when you planned the whole thing?''

He winced. "Kay, believe me. I never planned any of it. Maggie could have died any time, or been declared incompetent, or had a lucky accident. If I had the rights to her farm, even if she was still alive, there would be places, not banks, but other places, where I could get the money.

''I didn't know how to get Tony out of the picture. I hoped maybe I could buy him out for not too much, so I decided to tackle Terry first, while she was in town.'' For the first time there was an edge in his monotone. "I went to Terry that night, after Richie came back to the dance. I pretty much guessed where he'd been and I figured Terry would be in a good mood after her roll in the hay. I wanted to persuade her to sign over her interest in the farm to me. She was her usual bitchy self. I should have known it wouldn't work,'' he said scornfully.

I wondered if the scorn was directed at Terry or himself.

''She can't—couldn't—stand Maggie, didn't give a damn about the farm, and thought the land wasn't worth a red cent. She just wouldn't do it to spite me. She told me so. I even threatened to talk about her affair with Richie. She said 'Who cares?' Said I could rot in hell with my precious family before she'd give me a thing that wasn't mine. I just lost it. I went into a rage, started shaking her. Next thing I knew she was dead.

"That's when it came to me. If I could get Tony blamed for her death, I would be safe and they'd both be out of my way. There wasn't time to plan it all out, but I called the desk with that message for Tony."

"Didn't anyone realize, afterward, that it wasn't Terry calling?"

"They thought it was. She had a husky, cigarette-and-whiskey voice. I raised mine a little and slurred it a lot. Then I pulled out the phone cord, set the door lock, and put some gum in to jam it. Only a father of four would have a piece of gum in the pocket of his best suit. I left it open a crack so Tony could get in and hid around the corner. When I saw him go in I slammed the door, and that was that."

"Then you put the screws to that poor dumb twerp, Earl Mayhew, to provide some helpful details."

"You found that out? You're pretty good. That part was easy," Chris said, chillingly matter-of-fact. "He's a lot more scared of me than he is of LaForge."

I was tired, chilled, and scared, but I had to know the rest.

"It was you in the dark car the night Maggie was killed. Chief Smith was right all along."

"I never thought Maggie would work out her crazy plan with the Indians. I thought I had time to get control of the land," he said, almost plaintively. "I wasn't going to hurt her. She was old and sick, sicker than most people knew. I figured I could just let nature take its course, but when she said the new will would be signed the next day, I saw that I had no choice. You do see that, don't you? I really had to do it. She never knew. It was easy, Kay, so easy. She was lonely that night, and depressed. We were never friends, but I made up an excuse to drop in and she was ready to believe me. I talked her into a drink or two and after that, she was too confused to measure her insulin. So I helped.''

I saw the whole scene in a flash: Maggie collapsing; Chris saying he'd call for help, but actually waiting just out of the dying woman's sight for as long as it took; wiping his prints off the syringe and pressing her fingers onto it. I winced and Chris saw me.

''Not nice, is it? But she was old, Kay. She'd lived her life. Let her step aside for younger people.''

''Chris, I just don't understand it! Why did you think you had to do all this? You had everything.''

''But that's just the reason why,'' he said patiently. ''I was going to lose it all. If the business about the missing money came out I would have had to resign at the bank. I'd have disgraced my family. All those good works, all that respect, right down the drain. And I know I would have lost Sue and the kids. Even if they stood by me, they'd never feel the same way about me. Who would I have been then, broke, jobless, disgraced? Not Chris Campbell, that's for sure. A nobody. Worse, a jailbird nobody.

"Can you see me in jail? Oh, no, that wasn't going to happen to me. That's why I had to do it. Terry and Maggie didn't leave me with any other choice, and neither did you. Funny thing. I feel the worst about you. You're not old, like Maggie, or a bitch, like Terry. I wouldn't do it if I could find another way, believe me."

"There's just one thing," I said slowly, trying to stall for time. "I wrote up everything I know so far. It all points to you. Anyone who looks for me will find it in my room. And I mailed a copy to my office."

He looked at me thoughtfully, calculating. "My friend in D.C. called tonight with a story of an amazing coincidence. Just today, someone was asking about Fort Oake. I think it was you, and I doubt if you had time to make a copy of what you wrote. I don't believe you mailed anything." He stood up. "Give me your room key. I can get rid of all that stuff later." When I hesitated, he suddenly moved close, the gun in my ribs again.

"Come on, Kay," he whispered hoarsely, "you've got no choice. Get the key out and put it on the table. Now, on your feet. We've wasted enough time. I still have to sail the boat out, row back in the life raft, and drive back to town."

"And just when were you planning to shoot me?" I asked as he pushed me toward the dock.

"Oh, come on, Kay. Don't put it like that. If you weren't so damn nosy, or you'd said yes the other night, I wouldn't have to do this."

"You told me that I'd regret it." All the while I was thinking furiously that if I made a break for it, he might shoot me. If I didn't, he would certainly shoot me. And if I did, where could I go? I knew I couldn't outrun him.

My eyes were caught by the headlights from the car. Did that mean he'd left the keys in too? Maybe. It was a chance. The car at least would be some shelter. If I could push him down—run zigzag—it was really dark now, which would help. Oh, why didn't I keep up those long-ago karate lessons?

There were a few short steps leading from the lawn to the dock. It was now or never. I pretended to trip, making him loosen his grip on my arm for just a moment. I gave him a fast, hard, sideways kick with my high-heeled sandal. He lost his balance and fell, and the gun went flying off into the air. I was running across the lawn to the car, sobbing, when I heard tires squealing into the driveway and Tony's voice shouting my name.

I ran straight into his arms, gasping. "It's Chris. He may have a gun."

Tony pushed me down behind the car and knelt next to me. Chris was up now, limping across the lawn and shouting, "Tony, come out, you damn coward. I'll get you both now." He had found his gun. I saw it glinting in the light.

Without getting up and giving Chris a target, Tony shouted back, "Oh, no, Chris, not now. I called Al LaForge. He's on his way right now."

The shadowy figure on the lawn stopped moving. He said uncertainly, "I don't believe you. You're lying."

"Oh? Listen."

From very far away, we heard the faint whine of a police siren.

Chris cursed, ran limping to his car, and drove away so fast his tires sprayed gravel. I jumped up but Tony pulled me down again.

"We have to catch him!"

"What for? He's going to run right into the police. He doesn't have a choice. This road dead-ends at a dock in two miles. He knows that. He has to go toward the police. Maybe he thinks he can duck them but he can't. We can let them do their job. Now, what in God's name were you doing out here with him?"

"He made me. He had a gun. And you came in like the cavalry. I feel so *stupid*."

"It looked to me as if you were doing a pretty good job of rescuing yourself. What did you do to him?"

"I kicked him really hard and he lost his grip, and I ran like hell."

"Not bad. Were you running for the car?" When I nodded, he said, "I rest my case. Another minute and you would have gotten away, even if I never showed up. But I'm glad I did. I was afraid—"

His words were cut off by the sound of screeching brakes, metal crunching, glass breaking.

We jumped into Tony's car and drove down the road to where the police cars were clustered. Chris's car was off the road, sickeningly crumpled against a stone wall. The police officers were trying to get him out.

I ran to the car just in time to see them gently move his twisted, bleeding body to a blanket on the ground. He opened his eyes and seemed to focus on me. "Tell Sue," he gasped, "tell her I'm sorry." He closed his eyes again and an officer moved to check his pulse. Someone was radioing for an ambulance. Someone was doing CPR. By the time I walked back to Tony, I knew Chris Campbell was dead.

Tears streaming down my face, I put my head on Tony's shoulder. "It's all right," he repeated mechanically, as if to a child. "It's all right." Comforting phrases without meaning. "My cousin Chris. My *last* cousin." He shivered, then said sharply, "Kay, are you crazy? The guy tried to kill you. Are you crying for him?"

Sobbing too hard to speak, I nodded.

"It's all right," he said more gently, stroking my hair. "It's all right. You're crying for the Chris you used to know, aren't you?" I nodded again, still sobbing. "Sometime I'll tell you about the Chris I knew, the one who had to look perfect all the time, and it didn't matter at whose expense. Sometime. Not now. It's all right. Go ahead and cry."

The chief walked up to us. "I need to know what happened tonight."

"Not now, Al. Tomorrow. We'll come down tomorrow morning. I'm taking Kay home now."

TWENTY-TWO

THREE DAYS LATER Tony drove me to the airport in Syracuse. All the statements had been made, meetings taken place, my notes organized, clothes packed, good-byes said. The investigation of the deaths was virtually over, and I was needed in the office. I was going back to New York. It was time.

Tony and I had made our reports to Chief LaForge the morning after Chris died, but I saw the chief once more before I left. He called to say that a quick look at Chris's books had raised enough questions to keep the bank accountants busy for months. All the details of my story checked out. I was free to go, but would I stop by the office before leaving?

When I came in the chief said, "I owe you at least a thank you. You're a smart young lady, even if you sometimes do stupid things, and you're gutsy too."

"Thank you," I said politely. "Do you know what's going to happen next?"

"Not yet, not for sure, but I'll make a guess. I'm going to lay the whole thing out for Terry's folks. You know the truth, I know it, but all the evidence is circumstantial or basically hearsay, what *you* said *he* said. The guilty party is dead. Pursuing it further is only going to hurt the innocent: his folks, his kids, his wife.

And embarrass the entire family. If they want it dropped, I've got no problems with that. I'll wind up the case somehow. Don't know how yet, but I'll think of something.''

"Will you let me know?"

"Yes. And you'll bug me to death if I don't, won't you?" he said with the ghost of a smile.

"Of course I will."

"By the way, my friend at the bridge tells me they've got a line on Wishon and his friends. The old man is probably Wishon's boss's father-in-law. Used to be a very powerful mobster before he retired to Italy—without the option of reentry. There's a lot of men watching all known associates." He must have seen the gleam in my eye, because he added, "Yes, yes, I'll let you know about that too. So long, Miss Engels."

"Good-bye chief. Good luck."

During those last hectic days, Tony and I barely had time to see each other. He was frantically trying to gain on his neglected office work before his children were due to arrive. I was still researching small-town changes, squeezing in all the interviews I could before I had to leave.

I did see him, briefly, at Maggie's packed funeral, but he was too busy then to talk. He was doing the one last thing he could for her, taking the responsibility to see that she had the funeral she would have wanted. He gave the eulogy, vividly evoking the woman he had loved. He saw that all her friends, from many walks of life, were made welcome. He mentioned in his talk that she had once asked for joyous music at her funeral, and he saw to it that it was played. We heard some Gershwin, some of Beethoven's Ninth, and walked out to a Dixieland version of "Just a Closer Walk with Thee."

We managed to have one quick coffee-shop supper together. That was when he finally had a chance to tell me what brought him out to his cottage that night.

"It was Andy."

"No!"

"Yes. After I realized Chris had sent me on a wild goose chase, I knew something was very wrong, and I came flying back to town to try to find you. Andy was right here. He actually saw you leave with Chris, and followed you partway, until he got scared. He was standing at a phone in the lobby here, trying to decide if—if!—he should tell the police, if you can believe that. When he heard me asking about you, he told me instead. When he told me which way you'd gone, I guessed it must be my cottage."

"Andy! I can hardly believe it. I actually told him to quit following me. I guess I owe him an apology."

"Of course if he'd called the police right away, he would have saved you some scary moments. And if he hadn't seen me, I'm not sure he would have called the police at all. He seemed to be worried that they wouldn't listen to him." He grinned and I had to smile back.

"That's understandable."

"More than you know. They almost didn't listen to *me*! Al was not interested in my hunches about the cottage, but he did admit to being worried about you. After he told me about Mayhew, I raised hell with him. Told him he'd fry in the press if anything happened to you, and how happy I'd be to talk about how he refused to lift a finger. Once Andy finally told him a coherent story about Chris, and mentioned the gun, he moved pretty damn quick. Not as fast as I did, though. I must have broken all records, including my own best time, for that trip."

He suddenly started laughing. "Kay, I just realized something. That night, you were running to his car? Weren't the lights on?"

"Yes, he never had a chance to turn them off because I ran as soon as the car stopped and he was chasing me."

"So picture this: the poor bastard sails out to an island and rows all the way back. It's a good few hours work. And when he gets back, he has a dead battery! After all his careful plans, he finds he's stuck out there with no way to get home and no way to explain why he was out there. Imagine his face."

I did, and I laughed for the first time in days.

When we walked out of the restaurant, there was someone leaning against Tony's car, not moving, waiting patiently. It was Chief Smith.

"I was told you were looking for me."

"Yes," Tony said. "I left a few messages around."

"You know about Maggie." It was not a question.

"Yes, we know now. You were right. She was murdered. The man is dead. It is all about money and property. Do you want to know the rest?"

"Maggie was killed for property," he said bitterly. "No, I don't want to know the rest. What for? The details have nothing to do with me."

"Except for one. It looks like the farm will be mine now. I don't care about wills. I loved Maggie and I will respect her wishes." The chief nodded an acknowledgment and Tony went on, "You'll hear from me."

"I know. Maggie trusted you. Good-bye for now." He shook our hands and was gone.

I did see Andy one more time. He didn't have a phone, so I called him on his job and left a message, and he came by.

"Andy," I said, "let me buy you a beer while we talk. I owe you a big apology."

"I'd like the beer but it's on me. I've always wanted to take you out."

We sat in the hotel's lounge munching peanuts while I tried to thank him.

"Andy, I'm so grateful you didn't listen to me when I yelled at you, and so ashamed, too."

"I was worried about you, Kay. I saw you come back with your face banged up, and I knew someone was killed right here in the hotel. I watched out for you that night, in case they came back."

"That was you? I thought I dreamed someone was there."

He blushed. "I tried to tell you it was dangerous. I called to tell you it was dangerous."

"That was you?" I said again. "I thought it was a threat."

He looked embarrassed. "Maybe I didn't say it right, but I was worried, so I just kept watching whenever I could. I was scared when I saw Chris Campbell with a gun. I thought I could rescue you all by myself, but when I saw him go out into the country, with no one around, I thought, what if I can't do it alone? So I went back to get help."

"And you did get help."

He nodded, but looked troubled. "Do you think I should have gone to the police sooner? Right away? I thought they might not pay attention to me. Sometimes people don't."

"It doesn't matter," I answered. "Because you could tell Tony where we went, you probably saved my life."

"I was a help, wasn't I? I can be, you know."

"I'm so grateful that you were such a faithful friend, even after I wasn't nice to you. How can I thank you?"

"There is something," he said, his voice eager, but his face red with embarrassment. "It's really special."

I held my breath. I would do almost anything for him, but not quite everything.

"Would you send me a picture of you?" I let my breath out again. "I'd still like a real date, but I know you're going back to New York. So could you send me a new picture that I can have instead of the one I cut from the yearbook? I've kind of gotten used to your new haircut. And could you write something sweet on it? You know, so I can show the guys?''

''Oh, Andy, I'd be happy to. As sweet as can be.'' But taken in the office, I thought. Nothing romantic or sexy. I didn't want to encourage his dreams. ''Is there anything else at all I can send you?''

''Well,'' he said, hesitantly, ''I've always wanted a real Mets cap.''

''Consider it done.''

When we parted I shook his hand and then, on an impulse, gave him a quick kiss before I hurried away. When I turned back, just for a moment, I saw him still standing there, blushing red, with a big grin on his face.

The last person I had to see before I left was Sue. I couldn't leave without saying good-bye, but I dreaded the visit. Would she cry? Would the house be full of unpleasant relatives? And what could I possibly say?

As I drove into the driveway, I had a final thought that almost made me turn around. What if the children were there?

The house was quiet. My first thought was that no one was home, and I rang the doorbell hoping hard that it would be unanswered.

Sue came to the door. She looked like a different person, ten years older, pale, with dark circles under her eyes. Even her hair seemed to have lost color.

''I didn't expect to find you alone,'' I stammered. ''Am I disturbing you?''

"No, you're not," Sue said. "They're all over at my in-laws. I just came home for a rest. I wanted to be alone. Come in. I was hoping I'd see you."

"Sue, I don't know what to say. I'm so very, very sorry. If there's anything at all I can do—"

Sue looked straight at me and said evenly, "Chris was in some sort of trouble, wasn't he?"

I didn't want to be the person to answer that. I would rather have lost my voice right then and there, than have to answer that question, but Sue's steady, intense gaze gave me no choice. "Yes, he was. How did you know?"

"I've known for a while. When you've been married sixteen years, you just know, but Chris was always so protective. He could be leaned on, but he could never lean on anyone else. I know him. He thought he had to carry it alone. I *wish* he'd come to me!" she cried. Then she went on more calmly, "I've had two sleepless nights to work it all out. Tell me the truth now. I have to know. Was it really an accident?"

"Sue," I said slowly, searching for the right words, "I don't know. Maybe not. I think, right at the end, he was trying to protect you."

"Are you saying it would have been worse if he'd lived?" she asked with the same eerie calm.

"Maybe," I said. "Probably." I reached out and held Sue's hand tightly. "His very last words were 'Tell Sue I'm sorry.'"

Her eyes filled with tears but she brushed them away angrily. Chin up and head high, she said, "I may have to know it all eventually, but I'd rather not hear any more right now."

"Will you be all right, Sue?"

"Yes, I will. I have to be. I have four great kids who lost a wonderful father in an accident. I hope they never know more than that, because that's hard enough. I *have* to be all right."

"Is it too soon to know what you'll do?"

"Do? Stay here of course. Make a home for my boys. Whatever happened to Chris in the last few months," she said, her voice trembling, but her head still high, "doesn't take away from the rest of his life. I know that, and I'll make sure my boys, and everyone else in this town, knows it too."

Then she rubbed her eyes in a gesture of exhaustion and said, "I'd like to be alone now."

"Yes, of course," I said. "Please call if I can ever do anything, anything at all for you or your children." I offered her my card, and she put it down without looking at it.

"Good-bye, Kay," she said in a different voice. I left, filled with admiration and sure I would never see or hear from her again. The friendship that had sprung up so unexpectedly on my first day in town had been destroyed by the circumstances of Chris's death. Sue would never want to have anything to do with me again.

During the ride to the airport I told Tony about it and he agreed. "You'd always be a reminder of what she'd much rather forget. She's a tough lady, though, in spite of appearances. It took some kind of steel to ask you those questions. I'll check in with her every so often and keep you up-to-date on how she's doing."

Those words, with their assumption of a continuing relationship, seemed to hang in the air between us. We both let them linger there for a moment, before Tony said, "Kay, how will you write this story?"

"Damned if I know. I really don't see anything that could be gained by telling the whole story, and some very nice people could only be hurt. They're not public figures, after all. The whole world doesn't need to know about this. I guess I'm going to figure out some way of not doing it, just like Chief LaForge."

"Talk like that could get you thrown out of the press club."

"Oh, I don't know. I'm sure some of my esteemed colleagues would despise me for being a bleeding-heart wimp and say a story is all that counts. Some others would respect my sensitivity and ethics. I hope."

"I do. I have to admit I was afraid you might be a story-is-all person."

"I used to be. Maybe I'm just getting too old for this human interest racket. Maybe I'd better stick to politicians. There's less heartache. The part I hate most is that your uncle gets what he wants, after all—no story. That alone makes me want to write it, just for spite, but at least if I don't he can't kid himself into thinking it's because of him.

"However," I went on more enthusiastically, "I am definitely going to do something about the last two decades in small-town American life. I'm expanding it into a book proposal and I'm excited about it. I think it has possibilities."

"Sounds like that might require more visits back to Falls City," he said casually.

"Could be."

Tony kept his eyes on the highway but he put one hand out and gently covered mine. I laced my fingers through his and held tight for as long as he could drive one-handed.

At the airport we lingered over drinks until I had only a few minutes left to board.

"Kay, it's been one of the worst weeks of my life, but not without some compensations. Do we still have a dinner date next time I'm in New York?"

"I'd like that. I'd like it a lot."

"In three weeks then. Thursday."

"Good. Call me when you get in."

He hugged me hard; kissed me, tentatively at first, then quite definitely. Smiling all the way, I ran for the plane.

TWENTY-THREE

A WEEK AFTER I returned to New York I received an envelope in the mail. It contained three pieces of paper and a stiff little note.

> I could not think about this when I saw you, but you should have it. A few years ago, I helped out in my father-in-laws' office when he had an emergency, and I kept the keys, at his request. I didn't tell you this before, because I didn't want to raise false hopes, but I felt I had to help if I could.
>
> Sue

The papers were copies of documents, and one bore a notation: "Clients have requested we hold their file. They do not want file at home."

There were a birth certificate, an order of adoption, and an official letter of consent to an adoption. I couldn't believe my eyes. Before I could read them I had to pour a stiff drink and walk around my apartment twice. Meanwhile, those three pieces of paper sat on my coffee table, as ordinary as pieces of junk mail or office memos. At that moment, they looked like bombs to me.

My date and place of birth were what I had always thought them to be, but my birth name was Kay Osborne, my mother's maiden name. What could that mean? No father was given, but the name of the mother, and the signer of the consent letter, was Sally Osborne.

Sally? Was cousin Sally my mother? That explained the presents. Perhaps it even explained her gradual disappearance from our lives as I got older and could ask more questions.

These answers only raised new and frustrating questions. It just wasn't enough. I waited anxiously for the arrival of my parents' papers, barely able to work or sleep or eat until they did.

Federal Express finally delivered three large boxes, which I found waiting for me in my building lobby when I returned from work. I hauled them in, grabbed a pair of poultry shears—the first sharp utensil I could find—hacked them open, and dove right in.

There was so little there about my parents: high-school diplomas, inexpensively framed; my father's draft notice and discharge papers; laminated certificates marking their retirements from lifelong jobs. And yes, a gold watch for my father, with the date and "Thirty-five years of service" engraved on the back. My mother got a silver candy dish. Their marriage license, and a brass-framed wedding picture. I remembered the picture. My father, already balding at thirty-three, wore a dinner jacket that didn't fit, and my mother, with a matronly hairdo, was in an unbecoming brocade suit, with a big corsage. And they both had beautiful smiles. There were high school yearbooks and, tucked into my mother's, a prom picture with a boy who wasn't my father. No, of course not. They had married late.

There was a box with my mother's wedding ring, and the engagement ring with a tiny diamond chip, and the pearl earrings my father gave her for their twenty-fifth anniversary. And those were about all of the mementoes of their lives, except for an envelope with my birth certificate, the one I'd seen before, and an adoption certificate that only stated my name, Kay Engels, my parents' names, date and place of birth, date and place of adoption. All I learned was that I had been adopted at five days of age in Madison County. Without Sue's help I still wouldn't know anything about my background.

And then there were the two and a half other boxes that held every crayoned, glue-smeared, wobbly printed card I had ever made for either parent, every spelling certificate or writing award or science-fair blue ribbon I had ever won, every report card, and a whole folder of reports and projects. My senior-year term paper on freedom of the press was there, and so was my third-grade report, "The Camel, A Desert Animal." Every newspaper article that mentioned my name, and twelve years' worth of annual school pictures in a special frame. My graduation picture and my diploma, in matching silver frames. My christening dress, the blue satin costume from the one year I took ballet, and the tassel from my high-school graduation mortarboard, with its little dangling gold numeral that gave the graduation year.

I broke down then and cried for my parents, for the first time since my mother's funeral. I just kept thinking, "I never knew—I never knew..." and I sat there on the floor with my forehead resting on my arm, leaning against the glass coffee table, and cried until I soaked my arm and my shirt.

I was still sobbing on and off, in helpless fits, when I moved the last few items out of the box. It was a collection of odds and ends: papers relating to the sale of the Falls City house and the purchase of the Florida trailer, a notebook of my mother's favorite recipes, my mother's final medical records, an address book. At the very bottom was a small, very old leather bible with my grandmother's name embossed on the cover. Curious, I opened it, and found written inside the cover, in the old-fashioned way, a family tree. And next to my mother's name, crossed out but still legible, was written "Sally."

She wasn't a cousin. She was my mother's sister. That was the secret they had kept all those years.

My mother's sister. She must have been much like my mother, growing up in the same family and same town. No one exciting. No one unusual. Pretty ordinary, really. And yet, I remembered those extraordinary gifts in my childhood, and I wondered.

She was only seventeen when I was born. Was she working in a big town in Madison County, not too far from home? Had she become involved with a service-man from the air force base there? Or a married man? Or just some guy who took off when she said she was pregnant? Or had she moved there when she found out she was pregnant, to keep her secret? That her name was crossed out told me everything about her family's attitude.

So her older sister, childless after twelve years of marriage, took the baby. Took me.

Was she relieved? Grateful? Jealous? I wondered, with a pang, if she ever missed me. Had she willingly faded from my life, or had my mother made her? She was listed, and crossed out, four times in my mother's book. That told me that she moved a lot, and that they kept in touch. The last entry, in my mother's hand-writing, was in Florida, and was at least eighteen years old. Not much to go on, but maybe it could be a start.

My living room floor was covered with the contents of those boxes, but I ignored the mess for now and went to the refrigerator for some fortification. Choc-olate-chip ice cream would just about do it.

Then I went to my desk to do two things. I flipped through my Rolodex to find the names of any detec-tives I might have met, or any law enforcement offi-cers or lawyers whose experience might allow them to recommend someone. But before I started contacting them, I called my favorite restaurant to make a dinner reservation for my date with Tony. I wrote it carefully on the calendar and underlined it. Twice.

A SAFE PLACE TO DIE
Janice Law
An Anna Peters Mystery

First Time in Paperback

A DANGEROUS PLACE TO LIVE

For the rich and security conscious, Branch Hill offers the posh Estates—an exclusive community of impressive homes and a state-of-the-art security system.

Anna Peters and her artist husband arrive there for his gallery exhibit—but murder steals the show. The victim is a fourteen-year-old girl found bludgeoned near her home.

Anna quickly discovers the gilded Estates are a little tarnished around the polished edges. And when another death occurs, she begins to put together a complicated puzzle as tragic as it is terrifying.

"A sharp-eyed pleasant guide…along dark, peculiar paths." —*Publishers Weekly*

Available in October at your favorite retail stores.

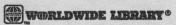

WORLDWIDE LIBRARY®

PLACE

Take 3 books and a surprise gift FREE

SPECIAL LIMITED-TIME OFFER

Mail to: The Mystery Library™
             3010 Walden Ave.
             P.O. Box 1867
             Buffalo, N.Y. 14269-1867

YES! Please send me 3 free books from the Mystery Library™ and my free surprise gift. Then send me 3 mystery books, first time in paperback, every month. Bill me only $3.69 per book plus 25¢ delivery and applicable sales tax, if any*. There is no minimum number of books I must purchase. I can always return a shipment at your expense and cancel my subscription. Even if I never buy another book from the Mystery Library™, the 3 free books and surprise gift are mine to keep forever.   415 BPY ANQ2

Name	(PLEASE PRINT)	

Address		Apt. No.

City	State	Zip

---

* Terms and prices subject to change without notice. N.Y. residents add
  applicable sales tax. This offer is limited to one order per household and not
  valid to present subscribers.

                                                                    MYS-94

Live To Regret
Terence Faherty

First Time in Paperback

An Owen Keane Mystery

LOST...AND FOUND

Ex-seminarian turned sleuth Owen Keane has been hired to look into the strange behavior of his friend Harry Ohlman, whose wife, Mary, was tragically killed.

While observing Harry during his retreat in a small seashore town, Owen can't resist the allure of Diana Lord, an enigmatic beauty obsessed by a death that had occurred there many years before.

But as Owen gets closer to the truth about Harry, he is forced to confront his own feelings for Mary and his unsettled score with his friend—as crimes of the heart, past and present, unfold in Spring Lake and a town gives up its secrets.

Available in October at your favorite retail stores.

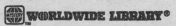

WORLDWIDE LIBRARY®

REGRET